To Kathy
One of the nicest people I have ever met.
Susie Honeycutt

Alfaland

By
Susie Honeycutt

PublishAmerica
Baltimore

© 2006 by Susie Honeycutt.
All rights reserved. No part of this book may be reproduced, stored in a retrieval system or transmitted in any form or by any means without the prior written permission of the publishers, except by a reviewer who may quote brief passages in a review to be printed in a newspaper, magazine or journal.

First printing

All characters appearing in this work are fictitious. Any resemblance to real persons, living or dead, is purely coincidental.

ISBN: 1-4241-3539-7
PUBLISHED BY PUBLISHAMERICA, LLLP
www.publishamerica.com
Baltimore

Printed in the United States of America

Dedication

To my adoptive parents, now deceased, Charles and Lulu Slabaugh, who gave me the love for the country and the farm, and to my natural parents Robert and Carrie McLaughlin, also deceased, for giving me life.

Acknowledgements

Thank you to my husband Jerry, for all of his love and patience, my son Kris, for his guidance, encouragement and words of wisdom, and to my brother Bob, for his support.

A special thanks to Darrell for the name Alfaland, to Nik for all his editing, and to Connie for the pictures.

Chapter One

Fort Akers Fire Chief, Claude Slabaugh, keyed up his car radio microphone. "Fort Akers dispatch-Fire Unit One rush traffic…request mutual aid from Elkhart County…we need at least four additional fire departments and request several more ambulances out at 27483 Patton Road. We've had a tornado touch down! We've received extensive damage!"

He'd never seen anything like this before.

"Chief," Fire unit three, Mickey Havert, shouted over the radio, "it appears Byron Patton's place has been hit hard." The voice became silent for a moment. "I sure hope they're in the basement."

Slabaugh called dispatch again, "Ft. Akers Fire Unit One…request you contact County Highway to see if they can help remove some of these tree limbs off of the road out here so the EMS can get through. Also, request you advise the Electric Co. that we have wires down all over the place. Tell everyone to use caution. Trucks ninety-five and eighty-nine, see if you and your men can get up to the Patton house on foot. We'll attempt to clear the drive."

Anxious minutes passed and a nameless voice responded urgently across the radio. "Chief," the voice said, "we have a female in the pool area. We need an ambulance up here as soon as possible. This place is a mess."

A section of the fence was removed by a neighbor, Jerry Honeycutt. He wrapped a heavy chain around it and pulled it with his tractor and the EMS and firemen rushed their ambulances and fire equipment through the pasture toward the farmhouse at Alfaland.

"Hurry!" a voice filled with adrenalin screamed. "Behind the house, in the pool, we need assistance."

Men raced toward the pool area. Advance Life Support Unit, Doug Anglin, had already entered the pool and was pushing away debris to get to the small figure at the bottom of the pond. He carried the young girl's lifeless body to the edge of the concrete pool. Several others assisted to lift her out and began to perform CPR. "Get an ambulance," one of them shouted. "We've got to get her to the hospital quickly. She does have a pulse."

A giant white ambulance backed around a tree limb that was stretched over the hood of a red convertible parked in the drive and then backed up to the pool area.

The rescuers heard frantic shouts coming from the bottom of the hill near a wooded area. When they turned their heads toward the shouting, the devastation besieged them. Strewn across the land and pond were tree limbs, pieces of fence, farm equipment and parts of buildings. Chief Slabaugh and other firemen ran in the direction of the plea.

"It's my wife, Leigh," Mr. Patton, the owner of the property shouted, the fear identifiable in his voice, "she's trapped!"

Chief Slabaugh analyzed the seriousness of Leigh Patton's condition. He spoke into his radio. "Does anyone have a chain saw? We need it at the edge of the woods by the south end of the pond area and check if we can get an ambulance down here."

Moments later a volunteer fireman dashed down the hill, carrying the chain saw. They removed enough of the tree trunk to pull Leigh out from under it.

Leigh's unresponsive body was loaded onto the stretcher and into the ambulance.

"I'm going with her," Mr. Patton said. He jumped into the ambulance.

"Byron," Chief Slabaugh held the door. "Before you leave, tell me how many were here. Who else should we be looking for?"

"My two daughters, Aimee and Kendra were up at the house, and my son-in-law, Aaron, was on the foot bridge," Byron said. "I'm not sure whether George, my hired hand was here yet or not. He would have probably been in the area of the barn."

The chief and the others standing with him glanced in the direction of the pond. The footbridge was scattered in pieces across the hill and in the pond. "We've already transported Aimee," he told Byron. "You get going. We'll find Kendra and Aaron and check for George." He closed the door and the ambulance rushed off.

Chief Slabaugh sighed, straining to keep his composure. He keyed up his radio. "All units, we have three subjects left, Kendra and Aaron Marshall and Byron's hired hand, George Truex, may be in the area of the barn. Kendra was near the house. Aaron was here in the pond area." He lifted his hat and wiped his hand across his forehead. He'd known the Patton family all his life. "Any volunteers start combing the area. Chuck, you guys start checking in and around the house."

"Hey, Chief, how's the Patton's?" a solemn response came back from assistant fire chief, Chuck Schmucker.

Chief Slabaugh hesitated before speaking "Byron is okay, but to be honest it doesn't look good for Leigh."

Assistant Chief Schmucker and several others began checking in the vicinity of the house. The back porch area and the kitchen had nearly been demolished. A dog barked. They stood silent for a moment to listen. "It sounds like he's in the basement," Schmucker said. "Let's clear this out and see if we can get down there."

In less then ten minutes, the debris was cleared away and the rescuers were able to get to the basement entrance and down the steps.

"She's here, it's Kendra." An eager female EMT, Stacey Stouder, kneeled beside Kendra Patton-Marshall. "It appears she's lost a lot of blood," she continued, "but she has a pulse and is breathing."

Kendra was lifted onto the stretcher, carried up the steps, and then placed into the ambulance. The dog, whose name is Buster, followed close behind them whining and attempting to jump into the ambulance with her. Jerry, their neighbor, walked over and took hold of the dog's collar pulling him back, "I'll take care of him, until they can get him." The ambulance doors closed just as it began to pour down rain.

"We have located Kendra, Chief. She's being transported to the hospital. She was unconscious but breathing." Chuck added, "There was quite a bit of blood at the scene." He massaged the back of his neck with his hand. "Where do you want us now?"

"We need to keep searching for Aaron." In his heart he believed, once more eyeing the shattered bridge, that it may be futile. "All available units and volunteers begin searching for Aaron Marshall. He was last seen on a foot bridge that was over the pond." They continued their search in spite of the rain.

At the hospital, Byron J. Patton sat quietly alone by his wife's bed. Dr. Jeff Scott, his dear friend for years, had agreed to give him the time he needed to be alone, as Byron had requested. He sat holding the mangled, bruised hand of his dead wife as he struggled within his soul to come to grips with the reality of all that was happening. They had been enjoying life with their girls just a little over an hour ago, and now here he sat. He wiped over his face with his mud-covered hand.

He rested his head on his wife's lifeless chest. Thirty years of precious memories flowed through his mind. He could not imagine what it would be like without her. Tears began to roll down his mud-spattered cheeks as he sat for several minutes silently speaking with his best friend, his God.

Byron at last stood to his feet and spoke to his wife, Leigh. "Those living are going to need me," he said. "I'll do my best; I make you this promise, my love." He repeated once more, "My love." He knew she would want him to take care of the girls. He touched Leigh's forehead with his fingers. She felt so cold. He stroked her blond hair. "I love you so," he said. Then he whispered, as if it were their unique secret, "I do know I'll see you again." He felt convinced that she heard him. It was almost as if he were attempting to comfort her. He leaned over and kissed her lips. "God, I'm going to miss you."

Mr. Patton stood with the determination of a soldier about to go to battle. He turned and walked from the room to locate his daughter, Aimee Sue, who was still unconscious. When he located her, the nurses were attempting to clean her up. She was covered with cuts and dirt.

Dr. Scott appeared by his side. "At this point," he said, "all we can advise you is that Aimee has no bones broken and doesn't appear to have any major internal injuries. Kendra has some broken bones and..." He hesitated, searching for the words. "I'm so sorry, but, were you aware that she was pregnant, Byron?"

Byron nodded.

"She lost the baby," Dr. Scott said. "I wish to hell this day had never been, Byron. I will do anything I can to help you and the girls."

"I know that, Jeff." He placed his hand on his friend's arm. "And I thank you."

"Kendra had just told us about the baby, maybe fifteen minutes before the tornado hit." He closed his lips and shook his head in disbelief. "We were all so thrilled. He grew quiet and stared down at the floor for a moment. "Is there any news on Aaron?"

"I haven't heard anything Byron. They were still searching for him the last I heard. I understand they did locate George in the barn and he was fine."

"I'm glad to hear that," Byron said. The girls are going to need me to be strong, And I will be." The two old friends then embraced. "Could you show me where Kendra is?" Byron asked.

Kendra Marshall was having a difficult time focusing but she could distinguish some people were near. She recognized her father. "Dad, is that you?" She began to smile. "What's going on?" Then, reality hit. "The tornado," she mumbled. "You're okay, thank God!" Kendra was relieved to see him. She felt she had to inform him, "Dad, I fell down the steps." Confused, she became silent for a moment as she stared at the wall contemplating, then fear gripped her voice. "Where's Aaron?"

Grasping for words, Mr. Patton stared down at his lovely daughter, but no words came.

She turned her head to look at him. Tears filled her eyes. "Where is Aaron?" she asked as dread swept over her.

Kendra's Aunt Jane came to his rescue. She walked over and stood beside Byron. "Kendra," she said, "they haven't been able find Aaron. They are still out at Alfaland looking for him."

Kendra stared at them both in disbelief. "How can this be happening?"

Her father, still not speaking, turned his head and walked over to the window. Kendra perceived he was weeping. She stared back at Jane for answers.

Jane wrapped her fingers around Kendra's arm, cleared her throat, and then spoke...the words seeming to stick in her throat, "Kendra, your mother...she didn't make it. She was trapped under a tree."

Heaviness descended on Kendra's heart. She could hear her father sobbing. Oh God no, she shrieked. "And, Aimee, where's Aimee?" she asked. "Is she all right?"

"She's still in the emergency room. They aren't sure how bad her injuries are," Jane said.

Kendra gave a sigh of relief.

"She was found in the pool unconscious," Jane continued, "and she still hasn't come out of it." Jane rubbed her hands up and down Kendra's arm. A stressed smile appeared on her face. "The medics probably would not have found you so quickly if it hadn't been for Buster barking."

"I remember him," Kendra said. She pondered for a moment. "He was licking my forehead." She looked into Jane's eyes. Her voice quivered. "There was blood all over my legs."

"I know," Aunt Jane said, stroking her forehead. She took Kendra's trembling hand in her own. "Apparently you were pregnant, honey, but you lost the baby." Jane struggled hard to remain strong. She knew they all needed her. She had no choice; she needed to do this for Leigh.

Mr. Patton came over and sat down beside her on the bed. He leaned over, took her in his arms, and held her as they both cried.

"What about Aaron," she asked, endeavoring to speak through her sobs. "Who's looking for him?"

Struggling to gain his composure, he answered, "The fire department, EMS, all our neighbors and several volunteers from town." He stroked her forehead and made a feeble attempt to smile. "We have a lot of people who care, Kendra."

"And Mom," her voice cracked. "What happened to her?"

"She was pinned under a large limb of a tree that had uprooted, honey," he stroked her forehead again. "They said she was killed instantly."

A nurse slipped into the room and gave Kendra a sedative. "We are going to have to keep her as quiet as possible," she stated.

"I agree," Mr. Patton said. He pulled up a chair and sat by her bed, holding her hand until she was released from the anguish of the day and drifted into a deep sleep. It was a pleasant welcome sleep, which brought back to life the beauty of the previous two days.

Chapter Two

Kendra's heart was pounding. She was getting more and more anxious to find out what Dr. Scott had to say. She had gone to her family doctor whom she'd known and loved since she was an infant. Numerous times over the years she had sat in Dr. Scott's office staring at the same beautiful oil seascape hanging on the wall of his office. She enjoyed the waves, the two rowboats and the sea gulls. The painting had a calming effect. "Maybe that's doc's intent," she laughed quietly to herself.

At last she heard the doctor's heavy footsteps coming down the hall and the door swung open.

He walked in grinning; his white teeth exposed under a grayish tan mustache. "I am sure you are not surprised to hear that you are pregnant, young lady," he said. "From the expression on your face, it is obvious that this is good news." He set himself on the corner of his desk. "Everything looks good. You're approximately three months along."

He advised her of the normal precautions to take and gave her a prescription for vitamins. Shaking his head in disbelief he said, "I can remember bringing you into the world." Kendra was moved and her eyes misted slightly when Dr. Scott walked around his desk, wrapped his hefty arms around her and then gave her a huge hug. "Congratulations," he said. "Your parents are going to be tickled I'm sure."

"I'm sure too," she agreed. Doctor Scott was a close friend with her father.

Kendra left the office and hurried home to finish packing for the weekend. Her and Aaron, her handsome husband of six months, had plans for a weekend get-away at Spring Mill State Park in southern Indiana.

Thanks to Joey, Aaron arrived home early.

Joey Dubious was their best friend and an assistant to Aaron at the *Fort Akers County Gazette*, the newspaper, which Aaron inherited after the death of his father during Aaron's senior year at Ball State.

Joey was a vigorous, dependable person at work who also poured his heart and soul into his band and Tae Kwon Do. He had a heart-piercing voice that mesmerized the audience whenever he sang. Kendra always had the notion that he would become famous someday, but Joey had never shown a desire to pursue that possibility.

"Great, you got off early!" Kendra was eager. "I have everything packed and ready to go." She kissed him. "Including Buster," she added. Buster was their gentle-natured German shepherd that Aaron had brought with him into their marriage.

They dropped Buster off at The Krazie Kutt, which was the beauty shop where Kendra worked. Carmon Pebble, Kendra's ambitious best friend and owner of the shop, was thrilled to keep Buster for the weekend. Kendra led Buster into the shop along with his food and doggie toys stuffed in a duffle bag.

Twenty-one-year-old Carmon had just finished taking payment for her last customer of the day. She walked around the counter and leaned her petite body over and hugged Buster. He appeared tickled about the arrangements.

"Your mother was in earlier this afternoon," Carmon said, "and she asked me to be sure to let you know, that they are having a barbecue on Sunday evening, if you get back in time. She sounded pretty anxious for you to be there. She also said your sister is home from college."

Kendra thanked her. She wished she could tell Carmon her good news, but she wanted to tell Aaron first. She hugged Buster and kissed him on the head. She wished Carmon good luck and was out the door.

The sun was a warm 80 degrees and there was not a cloud in the sky as the two lovers made the five-hour trip across Indiana. It was nearing dusk when they arrived at the lodge. "Let's hurry and get our luggage to our room so we can take a quick hike before dark," Aaron suggested.

They were able to get checked in and make it outside before dark. Aaron pointed, "Look our lodge is located on a steep ridge." He gestured to an opening between the shrubs where they could see a beautiful scenic view far below them. He discovered a path after walking a short distance. They followed the rugged path down to a large wooden footbridge stretching over a rapidly flowing stream.

Aroused by the aroma of her perfume and freshly shampooed hair Aaron stood behind Kendra with his arms secured around her waist. They watched the water rippling across the rocks in the stream.

"God, isn't this place peaceful?" Aaron whispered in her ear. "It makes a person just wish time could stand still right here." He kissed the back of her head.

Kendra turned to face him. She ran her fingers through his thick dark hair and down the back of his neck. "I love you," she said. Leaning against the rail of the bridge, she gazed into his dark eyes while grasping the back of his head and drawing him closer until their lips touched.

Aaron gently massaged the back of her neck. He stepped back and looked into her eyes. "You know, sweetheart, I've never mentioned this before, but I am so grateful that you saved yourself for me. What I have is rare; something that no one else has. That's special to me, honey." He kissed her again. "I never imagined that I could be this happy."

Kendra smiled. "You really need to thank my father for that more than me. I guess all of his preaching over the years sunk in. I'm glad I waited, too." She ran a finger across his lips. "Well, almost waited." She grinned and stroked his forehead with her fingertips. "You and I and God know I didn't quite make it. To tell the truth, I think I was more fearful of dad's reaction than God's."

Aaron laughed, "I know what you mean! But your parents are pretty wonderful people." His face saddened for a moment. "I wish my father was still around."

Their bodies were barely touching yet at the same instant an overwhelming desire come over them. Smiling, Aaron leaned over and kissed her exposed shoulder above her red-stripped halter-top. "I hope you're not too tired," he said raising his thick eyebrows up and down.

Kendra laughed. He reminded her of a little puppy waiting for dinner. It pleased her that he desired her so. She hoped he always would.

"Actually," he said, "I have dual motives for my desires." He caressed her dark hair that was dangling over her shoulder. "One, for the awesome pleasure of it, and, two maybe I'll get you pregnant. I'd adore having a little one running around the house."

She grabbed and hugged him, tears filling her eyes.

Her tears startled him; "What's wrong?" He placed his hands on her shoulders. "What is it? Kendra, did I upset you?"

She waved her hand in front of her, shaking her head, "No, No." Kendra's excitement made it difficult for her to speak. She blurted out, "I'm so glad you said that. I'm already pregnant."

Aaron stared at her for a moment, his eyes misting. He took her in his arms and held her. "This is fantastic, Kendra." He kissed her cheek. "How did I ever get so lucky?" He hugged her again. "I feel like celebrating or shouting."

They held hands and in the near darkness found their way back up the trail to the lodge.

The windows in their room were partially open when they entered and they could hear the harmonious sounds of the creatures in the park outside filling the night air.

"I can never get enough of you." Aaron said, while they embraced under the crisp white sheets.

Kendra sighed, "I feel the same way."

Contented, they fell off to sleep in each other's arms.

At daybreak, still embracing, the lovers awoke early to the cheerful sounds of a multitude of chirping birds outside their window. They showered together, ate a hearty breakfast, and then headed down a trail to locate an old restored village they had read about in the park brochure.

After hiking a mile, they discovered the village and began to browse through the many building which included an old tavern, drug store, leather shop and the old Griss Mill, where they purchased some freshly ground cornmeal to take back to her parents.

The one spot they both treasured more than all the others was the flower garden with its arched stone fence. It was filled with a variety of brilliantly colored flowers. They located a bench on the porch of what appeared to be the main log house overlooking the garden and, exhausted, they sat down to rest.

Kendra glanced around, "Just imagine there was probably a couple, just like us, that built this home long ago and sat right here where we are sitting. They must have seemed wealthy to their neighbors, at that time, having this fancy log house. It would have been exciting to live back then. Don't you think?"

Smiling, he gazed into her blue eyes and then leaned over to kiss her on the forehead. "If they'd have had what we have, they would have been rich."

Kendra's heart melted; he had such a unique way with words.

"I don't know, no computers?" he asked. "No TV, telephones, or cars. It would be weird. I'm pretty happy with the age I'm living in. It would have taken us days to get here in a buggy."

They both laughed.

Continuing their exploration they found themselves by a cool stream commencing from a cave that was high above them. The water so enticed them that they decided to take their shoes off and go wading. Aaron playfully endeavored to step from rock to rock and head to the opposite bank, but, he slipped mid stream on the wet rocks and fell into the icy water causing his bottom half to become soaked. Struggling to get up, he slipped and fell a second time.

Kendra couldn't hide her laughter. She placed her hands to her mouth. "Are you okay?" she asked.

"Go ahead and laugh. You would not believe how cold this is! I may never be able to have children again."

Kendra, fighting back the laughter, walked out on the rocks to where he was and made an effort to pull him up, but found herself on her knees in the freezing water also.

"It's freezing," she said.

"I'm cooled off, how about you?" Aaron laughed, after he had managed to crawl over the slippery rocks and out of the water and then help Kendra out as well. "Wow, that was cold."

"I feel crummy." Kendra felt her shorts. We must have looked like idiots to those people that walked by. I'm glad we didn't know them."

They removed their shoes and socks, wrung the water out of their socks, and carried their shoes.

"We'll dry quickly in this heat," Aaron said.

They continued on to see what else they could discover.

"Would you take a look at this?" Aaron said. They had located Hammer Cemetery and were reading the messages on the old tombstones.

"This is weird." He motioned for her. "Come here."

Kendra walked over to join him and read the haunting inscription on a small weathered stone. '*I ONCE WAS AS YOU, AND YOU SHALL BE AS I*' "That's creepy," she said.

"But true," Aaron said.

"I don't like it." Kendra shook her head and walked away. She didn't like to think about negative things. Why should she? Life was good. Kendra was the type of person who ignored or avoided anything she didn't want to deal with.

Still bare-footed, they found their way to the entrance of

Donaldson Cave. Kendra was exhausted and had to sit down. She sat on a large rock by the stream and put her wet tennis shoes back on while Aaron continued on to explore the cave entrance. She watched him investigate the entrance to the cave. He leaned over a rail exposing his long muscular legs and firm, slightly plump looking, rear end. "I love him so," she thought.

Aaron strolled back and sat down on the rock beside her. "Can we go back to the lodge?" Kendra asked. She stroked his dark tanned shoulder. "I'm really worn out."

Aaron placed his hand on her knee. "We shouldn't have gone so far. I wasn't thinking." He stood up and turned his back to her. "Hop on, I'll carry you."

"Aaron, you're kidding. You can't carry me," Kendra said.

"Get on," he ordered. "You are not heavy. I want to carry you."

Kendra jumped on his back, put her legs around his waist, and then secured her arms around his neck. He placed his arms under her hips and carried her all the way back to the footbridge they had visited on the previous night.

When they returned to the lodge, they confiscated a pair of reclining lawn chairs and sat by the pool for the remainder of the afternoon. Kendra napped while Aaron alternated between swimming and sun bathing. He couldn't seem to keep from smiling as he thought of the prospect of being a father. "Ah, life is wonderful," he thought.

They both felt rejuvenated when they went back up to their room to dress for dinner. Aaron sat on a chair with his feet cocked up on the bed and drank a soda, admiring his wife while she dressed. At age twenty-two, he believed Kendra to be the most beautiful woman he'd ever seen. He admired her long, dark auburn hair and soft blue eyes, which stood out even more with her part red, part tan face and freckles. Kendra's freckles had popped out as they always did when she was in the sun. He loved her petite little mouth and her rounded nose.

Kendra put her hair up on top of her head for the evening and slipped into a new light blue terry cloth strapless sundress she'd purchased for the weekend.

"You'd better quit looking so scrumptious," he said, "or I'm going to want to skip dinner and have dessert here shortly." He stared intently at her slim smooth hips and sunburned thighs, catching only a quick glimpse before she slipped the dress down over them.

"I'll help you out, honey buns." She leaned over and stroked his cheek and kissed the top of his head. "I'll leave so you can get dressed. I'm really hungry. I'm going down to the gift shop and look around." She slithered out the door, withering his desires.

Aaron soon joined her in the dining room. Kendra showed him a little log cabin box that she had purchased and how the roof opened so trinkets could be stored inside. "We have to have some memento of this weekend to keep," she said.

Aaron placed his hand over hers and squeezed it. "I agree."

They spent the entire meal discussing future plans concerning their lives and the new baby. "I know one thing," Aaron said stuffing the last bite of banana cream pie into his mouth. "We are going to begin looking at plans for a house as soon as we get home."

"Why don't we build on Patton Road?" Kendra said, "I know Daddy would gladly sell us some land near Alfaland."

"That would be perfect," Aaron said, "I've always thought that to be the most beautiful property in the world."

Later, when they strolled out onto the large stone porch of the lodge, the warm summer night was captivating. The sky twinkled with thousands of diamond like stars and the smell of the woods and pines and the perpetual sounds of the crickets and frogs surrounded them. Observing several families with their children come and go, enhanced the excitement they were feeling about their own future.

Nuzzled together on a single lawn chair, they sat in the dark under the blanket of stars for close to an hour before heading to their room for the night.

They did make one quick stop at the gift shop and purchased a little red tank top which had *SPRING MILL* printed in yellow on the front of it. "This will be our first baby purchase," Kendra said. "It is so tiny. I adore it."

"It's not much bigger then my hand," Aaron noted.

Aaron and Kendra again shared their love for each other on the final night of their mini vacation.

Aaron leaned up on his elbow; his leg draped over her thigh, and stroked her face with his hand. "I'm excited about becoming a father." He rested his hand on her abdomen. "It's so fantastic to think my son, or daughter, is in there. It's all so wonderfully mind boggling."

Lying in the dark, her thoughts wandered back to what Aaron had said on the bridge the evening before, about wishing he could just make time stand still and hold on to the moment. "We don't have to hold on to just this moment, we have so many more to look forward to."

Chapter Three

Kendra and Aaron picked up Buster around three in the afternoon and headed out to Alfaland, the one hundred and eighty-eight acre farm where Kendra and her sister Aimee were born and raised. Kendra held countless cherished memories of her life growing up at Alfaland. It had been difficult for Kendra to give up that part of her life when she'd married and moved to their small apartment in Fort Akers. Alfaland, located five miles northwest of Fort Akers derived its name from the word Alfalfa, which was given to the farm by Kendra's grandparents, Pebble and Ora Patton, after they were married in 1922. They sold Alfaland to Kendra's father soon after Kendra was born. Byron J. Patton farmed Alfaland his entire life until his recent retirement. Her grandparents, who now live in Florida, come back to Indiana only a couple of months each summer.

Byron and Leigh shared a deep love for their daughters. Not only did they work hard together as a family but they played hard together as well. Winters at Alfaland were filled with skating and sledding and summers were likewise brimming with activity. If there was a problem, they talked about it. They read the Bible together often and discussed the meaning of its message and prayer was a central part of their lives.

In the back seat, Buster began to settle down from his excitement over being reunited with his family. The red Cavalier convertible passed the half-mile long stretch of woods, rounded the curve in the narrow gavel road and came upon the white rail fence bordering the eastern perimeter of Alfaland.

Kendra glanced beyond the fence and saw Patience, her black Arabian mare, lift her head, point her ears forward and then gallop off through the grassy pasture arching her tail slightly.

Slowing down in order to make the turn into the driveway, Aaron noted the dark sky off to the west. He continued up the half-mile long drive that was shaded with numerous old beech trees and pines. "I hope the rain holds off till we eat, I am starved."

Kendra shifted her eyes from the pasture to her husband's muscular arm just below the rolled up sleeve of his t-shirt and said. "I'll never forget this weekend."

Grinning down at her, Aaron took his hand and squeezed the cap of her sunburned knee. "Me neither," he said.

He pulled around to the south side of the circular drive and came to a stop. Kendra spotted Aimee Sue, her younger sister, who had just returned home for the summer after completing her second year at Indiana University, running up the path from the pond to greet them. Watching Aimee running toward them barefoot, in her old, gray, baggy sweatshirt and blue jean cut-offs, Kendra's mind flashed back to their childhood. Kendra's parents waved at them from the gazebo next to the pond where they were busy preparing dinner.

Kendra, along with Buster, who didn't wait for the door to be opened but jumped over the side, raced to meet Aimee.

"It's so good to see you," Kendra wrapped her arms around Aimee's petite body while Buster raced in circles around them yipping and wagging his tail. "I've missed you. It's been so long since you've been home, too long." She embraced her again.

"I know," Aimee said, "I've had so much going on this year."

Aaron caught up with them. "Hey girl, how's it going? You are looking good."

"Can I assume you are you still taking good care of my big sister?" she asked.

A quick glance ensued between Kendra and Aaron.

"He's taking care of me all right," Kendra said. "As a matter of fact he's given me your little niece or nephew to carry around."

Aaron smiled, shook his head in amusement and slight embarrassment and then continued on toward the pond with Buster, leaving the two to catch up talk.

"You're going to have a baby, I can't believe it," Aimee said. "This is fantastic. I have some good news for you too. I'll tell you later," she said as they walked, arms interlocked, down the hill and joined the family.

Their father, Byron, looked at them and smiled as he flipped the hamburgers that were cooking on the grill. "It's sure a pleasure seeing the two of you together again. Somehow you both look like you're up to no good already." He laid down the spatula and walked over to embrace them. A more serious tone took over his voice. "I miss you both," he said. His eyes glassed over as he fought back the lump that came into his throat. His voice cracked. "Your mother and I think of you everyday."

"Dad, we're grinning about the fact that you and mom are about to become grandparents!" Kendra proudly announced.

"Oh honey, that's great. I'm thrilled!" Kendra's mother, Leigh Patton, dried her hands and rushed over to embrace her older daughter. "I'm so ready for a baby in this family." She paused a moment, tightening her lips together, "Even if that does make me a grandma." They all laughed.

Byron turned to shake Aaron's hand. "You have a babysitter here anytime you need it. I can't wait to spoil the little dumpling."

"So how are you doing? Leigh asked, "How far along are you?"

"I'm feeling great." Kendra said. "No problems. I just get a little tired once in a while. Dr. Scott said we should have the little blessing shortly before Christmas. That'll be a pretty special Christmas present I'd say. Wouldn't you?"

The three women continued discussing nursery plans, baby showers and names while helping put the finishing touches on dinner. "I vote for Ian if it is a boy and, of course, Aimee, if it's a girl," Aimee said. They all laughed.

"Did you and Aaron have a nice trip?" Leigh asked.

"Incredible. It's just as beautiful as ever at Spring Mill. It was a perfect weekend." Kendra glanced over at Aaron, who was standing with her father. She then walked over and put her arm around her mother. "I believe I've found what you and Dad have," she said.

Leigh leaned over, kissed her oldest daughter on the cheek, and then rubbed her hand over her back. "I couldn't ask for any more than that for you girls," she said, "Aaron is a good man."

At age forty-five, Leigh was still an attractive woman, with her soft blond hair and blue eyes. She was the only one in the family that had a light complexion. The girls both had their father's darker skin and hair except Kendra did have her mothers blue eyes. It took a lot to get Leigh upset. When emergencies arose, she was the calm one in the family. She rarely lost her temper and she would do anything for the girls. But, even so, she had her rules and enforced them which caused Kendra and Aimee to feel she was too strict and protective. Leigh felt it had paid off after seeing the way they had turned out. She placed the plastic cups on the table. "Can someone run up to the house and get the iced tea?" she asked. "It's on the kitchen counter."

Nodding toward Kendra, Aimee said, "We'll go."

Kendra nodded in agreement, grabbing a couple of carrots off the table, for the trip. "This will give me a chance to find out what Aimee mentioned she wanted to tell me," Kendra thought to herself. They headed up the hill in the direction of the house.

Enjoying the country air, Aaron inhaled a deep breath and strolled out onto the small footbridge that Byron had built over the pond. "It's so peaceful here," he said to Byron, who joined him.

Mr. Patton shouted in the direction of the girls, "You two get moving so we can eat before this storm moves in. It appears to be moving in fast."

Kendra whirled around and shouted back. "We'll try. I'm famished. I have to eat for two now, you know." A sudden serge of pride flowed over her. She was married to Aaron Marshall! Silently she recalled their previous evening together.

Aaron Marshall grinned and waved back at his wife.

Kendra and Aimee entered the kitchen through the back porch. Buster slipped in with them just before the door closed. "Okay, what is it you have to tell me?" Kendra asked.

"I have some extraordinary news," she said. "I am in love. He's the most charming and wonderfully handsome man I've ever met. I appreciate now how you feel with Aaron." Aimee paused a moment and caught her breath. "He melted my heart from the first moment I looked into those beautiful blue eyes. I believe it was fate the way we were thrown together last winter. In the middle of a blizzard, would you believe? We both knew immediately that we were meant for each other. I've never meant anyone like him."

Kendra had never seen her younger sister like this. "This guy must be really something special," she thought. "Sounds like love to me," she said feeling a little reservation as she hugged Aimee. Kendra knew that Aimee could be impulsive at times, but she didn't want to dampen Aimee's apparent happiness by indicating any concerns. It was difficult for Kendra to imagine Aimee as anything other than the bubbly little "Tom Boy" she had played with as a child. "I truly wish you as much happiness as Aaron and I have," Kendra said. "So tell me more!"

"I really love him, Kendra. I know I've found the man I'm going to spend the rest of my life with," Aimee said. "And he feels the same." She stepped back and looked Kendra in the eye. "He's asked me to marry him this summer and I'm going to do it. I can't wait to have a baby like you. I'm just so happy; I feel like my heart could just explode. You are going to love him, too. I want you and Aaron to meet him next week. I'm inviting him to come here and meet the family. Kendra, he is absolutely gorgeous. He has the most beautiful blond curly hair. Sometimes it drives him crazy, but I love it!"

Kendra laughed and placed her hands on Aimee's shoulders.

"Slow down," she said. "What is his name?"

They were interrupted by the ringing of her parent's cell phone on the table.

Aimee answered it. "It's Aunt Jane," she said while listening with her hand cupped over the mouthpiece. "No we haven't." Aimee displayed slight concern in her voice. "We've been down by the pond. Sure, hold on, I'll get her."

"She says there is a tornado warning for our area," Aimee said. They were used to watches and warnings in their area, so they didn't get too excited. "I'm going to run the phone down to Mom. She so desperately needs to speak to her." Aimee rolled her eyes. "I'm sure Dad is going to want to move inside. You know Dad. He takes these warnings seriously. You can just stay here." She headed out the door with the phone.

Returning from the bathroom, to the kitchen, Kendra could hear hysterical shouting in the distance. Terror gripped her. Her family was shouting from the bottom of the hill. Kendra rushed to the back door and saw Aimee racing toward the house, panic on her face.

"Get in the basement!" Aimee shouted.

Kendra's eyes then lit upon it. To the southwest, behind the woods, extending from the clouds to the ground and throwing debris through the sky was a huge whirling black cloud. There was too much dirt in the air to make out anything toward the pond. Kendra stood petrified as Aimee breathlessly raced from the far side of the swimming pool toward the back door. "Get in the basement," she screamed again.

The air around them became still.

Kendra whirled around and then ran toward the basement door. Every nerve in her body was filled with horror but she managed to pull the basement door open. When she started through the door she could hear an amplified roar, similar to that of a freight train, engulfing the house. The basement door slammed against Kendra's back, forcing her airborne over the stair steps. She groped for the railing. She could see herself flying toward the basement floor. Kendra landed on her left side, her arm stretched out past her head on the steps near the bottom of the stairs.

She was conscious that Buster was standing over her on the steps, whining and licking her forehead. Excruciating pain shot through her left shoulder, and Kendra realized that she couldn't move it. She managed to drag herself the three additional steps onto the concrete floor of the basement.

Kendra's eyes began to focus. She was startled by the display of blood covering the wooden steps above her. She twisted her head and saw a large amount of blood covering her blue jeans. She wondered where all the blood was coming from.

Dread pierced her soul when she remembered Aimee, Aaron, and her parents outside. An isolated tear rolled down each of her tan and freckled cheeks as she lie there with her face plastered against the cold, damp concrete. Several minutes passed. Kendra could faintly detect unfamiliar voices shouting off in the distance, along with numerous sirens, before the darkness consumed her and she surrendered to unconsciousness.

Whimpering, nervously Buster paced back and forth numerous times before lying down beside her. He whined and nuzzled his cool nose up against the long dark hair that was sprawled out across the concrete behind Kendra's head.

Chapter Four

Kendra opened her eyes. She was instantly walloped with extreme pain throughout her entire body. Her arm had been broken in two places, along with a broken shoulder and hip. Due to hemorrhaging, the doctors felt it necessary to internally pack her in order to stop the bleeding. It was painful to turn her head.

The further alert she became, the more she was forced to face the reality of the previous day. The nightmare flooded back into her mind. "Oh God," she said, "Please help me, I can't face this."

Kendra saw Joey sitting across the room. When he noticed her eyes had opened, he walked over and took her hand in his. He was trembling, and it was obvious from his eyes that he had been crying.

She clenched his hand and held it close to her face. "Have you heard anything about Aaron?" Kendra asked.

Carmon was also there, and she walked over and stood next to Joey. They had been sitting by Kendra's bed for the last two hours waiting for her to wake up. Her father had gone into another room about half an hour earlier to rest.

Joey nodded. "Yes we have." He paused for what seemed like a minute. He felt ill. "I'm so sorry, Kendra, but Aaron was found in the pond." He hesitated again, tears filling his eyes. "There was nothing anyone could do to save him, Kendra."

Kendra never knew this kind of pain existed. Sorrow, injury, catastrophe and death were not words that existed in her world. She felt numb.

An older nurse, unnoticed by Kendra, walked into the room and gave her a shot to ease the pain, and to keep her still.

Mr. Patton and Jane came into the room. As soon as they saw Kendra's face, they realized that she had been told about Aaron. They went to the opposite side of the bed from Joey and Carmon. Her father laid his large hand over Kendra's left hand, which partially protruded from the huge cast that was over her entire left arm.

The darkness that Kendra felt was unbearable. With her other hand she took Joey's hand and held it against her tear-covered face and sobbed until the sedative the nurse had given her let her escape back into sleep.

Kendra's injuries forced her to be confined to her hospital bed for two weeks, which made it impossible for her to attend Aaron's or her mother's funeral. Lydia Ann, who was the seventeen-year-old daughter of one of their Amish neighbors sat with Kendra on the days of the funerals so the others could attend.

Friends and family made arrangements to take turns sitting with Kendra and Aimee for the first couple of weeks. The grief of losing Aaron, her mother, and the baby, they felt, was a dangerous combination for Kendra.

Faithful friends, Carmon and Joey, spent every free moment with her that they possibly could. Joey was there every night and weekend. With the exception of Kendra, Joey felt the loss of Aaron more than anyone else. He had been Aaron's best friend. He took it upon himself to make sure operations at the *Gazette* continued to run until Kendra was able to decide what she wanted to do.

Fifteen days after the tragedy, Kendra's heart was sick when, for the first time, Carmon rolled her in a wheelchair to Aimee's bedside.

She was startled to see the passion for life and enthusiasm that had radiated from Aimee just days before had disappeared. Before Kendra now was a frail, thin, motionless body that appeared to be asleep.

Dr. Scott and other specialists were unable to give any guarantee that Aimee would ever come out of her coma. While still hospitalized, Kendra spent every available moment with Aimee. Sometimes she would just talk to Aimee, believing that her words were being heard. Other times, she would read to her or play the radio and CDs. Dr. Scott had indicated that there was a good possibility that Aimee was able to hear her.

The day Kendra was to be released from the hospital was not necessarily a happy day for her. Her heart was heavy as she sat on the edge of her bed waiting for her father and Aunt Jane. "Where do I go?" she thought to herself. "Nothing is ever going to be the same again. Go to Alfaland, without Mom, or home to the apartment, without my precious Aaron." Her eyes began filling with tears, as they had done often the last several days.

Mr. Patton settled the question by informing her they were taking her to Alfaland for a while. In his heart, he was hoping she might decide to stay.

On their drive out to Alfaland the evidence of the tornado was visible throughout the countryside. There were trees uprooted, barn roofs missing and trailers overturned.

At Alfaland things were almost back to normal except for some debris still scattered in the fields. Thanks to all the neighbors and friends, the kitchen roof and the back porch had almost been restored. All it needed was to be painted. The only building that had been destroyed was the pole barn, between the house and the barn, which Mr. Patton had used for a garage and shop.

Kendra never realized that there were so many good, caring people around her. It warmed her heart to hear of all the concerned friends and expressions of love and kindness that people had shown her family.

Kendra was pleased when Aunt Jane had decided to move out to the farm with her and her father. Lydia Ann had been doing a terrific job of attending to things at Alfaland, but it was a lot of work to put on a young girl. Due to the fact that Jane's home was several miles away, and with her visits to Kendra and Aimee everyday and now caring for things at Alfaland, it made things much easier for her. It was odd how Jane had this way of tilting her head when she spoke, just like Leigh always did. She also, just like Kendra's mother, had a knack for organizing and decorating. She even looked a lot like Leigh except Jane wore her hair short and it was darker then her mothers, more of a strawberry blond. Jane, who had never married, had traveled to locations such as Ireland, Alaska, and Israel during the summers when she wasn't teaching school. She had been an elementary teacher for years at the Ft. Akers Elementary School.

By July, Kendra's physical wounds were almost healed. She was now feeling the desire to move back to her apartment and attempt to get on with her life. Joey had agreed to come and pick her up the next afternoon after he closed the shop.

On the day she was to leave Alfaland, Kendra felt drawn to take a walk down to the pond. She had put it off the entire time she had been there. It was a warm sunny afternoon and everything appeared about the same except for the fact that the footbridge was no longer there. It was a beautiful serene spot amid the green grass, the pond and the woods. Birds were chirping and horses were grazing at the top of the hill in the field to the south of the house. It was hard to visualize the tragedy that had occurred there a few months earlier. Kendra stood staring into the tranquil water for several minutes. Her heart ached. Her dreams were shattered. Her mind drifted back to her and Aaron's final moments together at this spot. She recalled turning and admiring him as she had walked up the hill with Aimee and how he had smiled and waved at her that last time. She was thankful that she'd had that last weekend at Spring Mill with him to hold in her heart. "It's like some unknown hand has erased my future," Kendra thought. "There is nothing, nothing but memories." She so desired to be held in his arms one more time.

Kendra sat down on the grass beside the pond and put her arms over her knees. She tucked her head in her arms and whispered. "Oh, Aaron, I don't want to go on without you."

She heard a noise behind her. It was Joey. He walked over and sat down beside her in the grass. Without saying a word he put his arm around her and held her against his shoulder.

"Joey what am I going to do?" she asked.

"You'll make it, my friend. Just try to concentrate on one day at a time and draw upon that inner faith in God that you've always had."

"I've never really had to use it. It's easy to have faith, Joey, when everything is going beautiful. Everything has always been so perfect in our family. Nothing bad has ever happened, until now. I haven't lost my faith in God, but I'm just so overwhelmed with sadness I'm unable to think about God. Do you know what I mean?" she asked, "I'm just so sad, Joey."

"I know, Kendra. Sometimes God has a different road for us than we planned. Remember Job? How he lost everything, but in the end he ended up with more than he'd had in the beginning."

"I never thought about that. All I remembered was how he lost everything. I can't imagine things being any better then they were before. I can't imagine everyone being happy again." She looked at Joey and smiled. "I don't know what I'd have done without you, Joey."

"Come on, my friend." Joey smiled. "Let's take the first step. I'll take you home."

Chapter Five

Kendra sat with her chin resting on the back of her cream-colored leather sofa. She had been staring out the window, watching a little girl riding a tricycle around on the sidewalk along the front of her apartment.

The last few weeks since her move back to the apartment had been difficult. At times, she felt her life was over at age twenty-two. "Without Carmon and Joey, I'd never have made it," she thought," but I can't depend on them forever." Carmon had even spent the previous Saturday night at Kendra's apartment. Kendra was well aware that Carmon had been making things up for them to do just to keep her busy. She appreciated Carmon's efforts, and tried to enjoy herself, but found it difficult for her to put her heart into anything she did.

Alone on this Saturday evening, Kendra was having one of the worst moments that she'd experienced since Aaron's death. She had come across the little red tank top she and Aaron had purchased from the gift shop at Spring Mill. Her loneliness was unbearable, making her restless, fidgety, and nervous. She had to do something.

Carmon was out of town for the weekend so she decided to phone Joey's house to see if he was home. It rang three times. She started to hang up, but then put the receiver back to her ear one more time. Joey answered after a couple more rings

Kendra started to speak, but lost control and broke down crying.

"Kendra, where are you?" Joey asked. "Are you at home?"

"Yes," she managed to say through her sobs.

"I'll be right there, you hang on," he said.

Joey turned to the pretty young blond, Julie McLaughlin, sitting on his sofa. "I am sorry; we are going to have to break this up." He walked to the closet and got their jackets. "I have an emergency."

"You're going over to Kendra's," she said, reluctant to move. "That's no emergency."

"Yes it is," Joey said while he helped her with her jacket. "I'll do anything for Kendra to help her get through this."

"This gets a little old Joey," she grumbled.

Within twenty minutes, Joey was ringing Kendra's doorbell. He could hear Buster barking inside. Kendra opened the door. She grabbed him around his shoulders and cried. He put his arms around her and held her.

She showed him the little red shirt clenched in her hand. "We bought this at Spring Mill for the baby."

Joey gave Kendra the precious gift of just listening. She talked about Aaron and the baby plans they had made, about building a house out at Alfaland and the weekend at Spring Mill. She spilled her heart out to him and cried for two hours.

The clock was chiming nine o'clock when Joey made a suggestion. "Let's go somewhere. I'll take Buster out while you freshen up and we'll get out of the apartment for awhile."

Kendra was hesitant at first, but she looked at Joey for a minute and then agreed. "It would feel good to get out." She washed her face, put on a little make-up and then slipped into a pair of jeans, a white tank top and her denim jacket.

Kendra had no idea where they were going, but she was already feeling better. He took her to a restaurant/night club on the north side of South Bend. They ordered a couple of burritos and drinks. There was an upbeat band, and Kendra was starting to feel somewhat rejuvenated.

"This was a good idea." Kendra smiled at Joey. "Thank you, Doc Joey. You are such good medicine for my soul." Sitting across the table from him, Kendra perceived what a handsome man Joey was with his dusty blond hair and mustache that highlighted his charming smile. "So why has no one nabbed you yet, Joey?"

"I don't know. I guess I'm too particular. Julie and I've been dating for a long time. She's a wonderful person." His face saddened somewhat and he glanced down at the drink in his hand. "It just seems there should be more to a relationship than what I feel." He looked up at Kendra. "I'm waiting for the real thing but maybe it won't ever come."

"The real thing is worth waiting for, Joey."

They finished eating their burritos and ordered another drink. The band began to play, "Unchained Melody."

"Let's dance," Joey suggested. "We'll take it real easy," he said, "I know you're still recuperating."

Joey held her close while they danced the entire song without a single word. "I wish so desperately I could remove the sorrow for her," Joey thought to himself.

We better sit awhile," Kendra said after they danced to the second song. "I guess I'm still a little out of shape."

They returned to their table. "So, how is Aimee doing?" Joey asked.

"No change," Kendra said. "We all take turns spending time with her but its pretty depressing."

"And, your father, how is he doing?" Joey asked.

"He's doing well. He is a strong man, but," she hesitated, "he's depending on Aunt Jane an awful lot. Jane can't go on like this. She's going to have to get back to her own life soon. She has been giving so much of herself to all of us."

"She seems to be a pretty terrific person," Joey said. "Doesn't she have a husband and family? I would think they would be missing her."

"No, she never married. She seems to enjoy taking care of us."

"I see one of our old favorites, Joey Dubois, is here tonight!" a gentleman at the microphone announced.

Joey smiled at the man.

"Joey," he asked, "could we talk you into sharing a song with us? It's been a long time. We've missed you and your band around here."

Joey lifted his hand in a negative response and shook his head at the man, but quite a few in the crowd began to applaud.

"Oh, come on, Joey, I'd love to hear you sing again." Kendra tipped her head to the side and touched his arm. "Please."

Staring at her, he hesitated for a moment but then agreed. "Only for you." He smiled.

He spoke a few words with the band and then took the microphone. "I'm here with a dear friend tonight," Joey announced, "and there is a song that I think would be nice for her to hear. This is for Kendra." He glanced at her and gave a slight bow.

Kendra listened while he sang an old song she'd always loved, "Yesterday." "How well it fits," she thought. "Yesterday, all my troubles seemed so far away." she sang along.

Captivated by Joey's unique voice, the patrons in the room fell silent.

"He's so exceptional." Kendra wondered if maybe Joey had missed his calling in life. "It's such a waste for only a small number of people in this world to ever hear his extraordinary voice," she thought.

The audience was delighted and displayed it with enthusiastic applause.

"Your voice is so beautiful and that song was perfect," Kendra said when he came back and sat down at the table. "I hated for it to end. Your singing just seems to flow out of you. You ought to make a recording some time."

He smiled, "Thanks, I do enjoy singing." He paused. "But, the truth is, I'm really not a people person. I don't like crowds. If I could just stay at home and make recordings, it would be great." He grinned, took a sip of his drink and then leaned forward in his chair to look her in the eyes, "I don't think that would work, do you? Besides..." He leaned back in his chair. "...I just don't like all the stuff that goes with it. I guess you could say I'm a loner. Not that I don't love people, though." He smiled. "Just not all at once"

"Are you still singing with the band?"

"I haven't for quite sometime because I've been so busy with the paper. I haven't done much of anything lately. I rarely even get to my martial arts classes anymore."

Kendra became conscious of how much responsibility he'd had with the paper. She'd been so wrapped up in her own grief. She hadn't even thought about it. "Maybe you should hire some help," she suggested.

He stared at her for a moment and then grinned. "Kendra, you're the boss."

Kendra stared at him for a moment. "I guess so," she said. "With everything that's been going on, I haven't even thought about the paper. I can't believe I'm so ignorant. Why didn't you say something?"

"We all felt it was best to just give you some time before discussing anything," Joey said.

Kendra placed her hands over her cheeks, "Oh, Joey, I can't handle that." She shook her head. "I don't know the first thing about publishing a paper."

"You can learn," he said.

"Joey, would you consider taking over as manager of the paper for me?" She reached over and put her hand over his arm. "Which, actually, you already are," she said. "We'll set up the arrangements next week. You are the only person that could do it and that I can trust. You say what you need financially, or whatever, and you've got it. If you do that, I'll keep the paper for now." She squeezed his arm. "I don't really want to jump in and sell it right now."

"I was hoping you'd feel that way." He took a sip of his drink. "I didn't want to say anything. I wanted to give you some time."

"You know what? Maybe I'll even go back to school," Kendra said, "take some courses in journalism and business." She was beginning to feel alive again, like there was a future for her.

"Way to go." Joey smiled.

Joey and Kendra danced a few more times and then left for home. It was shortly after one o'clock. During the drive back to Ft. Akers, Kendra felt more optimism than she had in a long time. It had been nice to step out of the world of sadness that had engulfed her for so long. She found herself chattering and even laughing.

"This feels so good. Joey, I really enjoyed myself tonight." She looked over at him, "Thank you, what would I ever do without you?"

"I'm glad, my friend. That was the whole idea."

Buster was all over them when they arrived back at the apartment, as usual. Kendra was thankful she still had Buster. He was a good companion and he somehow made her feel closer to Aaron.

"Will you be all right now?" Joey placed his hands on her shoulders.

"Yes, I'm much better thanks to you, Joey." She reached up, gave him a lengthy hug, and kissed him on the cheek. "You've been more help than you'll ever know."

He held her in his arms for several moments. "You call me anytime," he said. He placed his fingers under her chin. "And I mean *anytime* you need me. I'll be here in a flash."

The following week, Kendra and her father made arrangements with their lawyer to give Joey complete authority over the business. Joey hired an assistant and a secretary within the week.

Finances were not going to be a problem for Kendra due to the insurance money Aaron had left her. The paper was also profitable. Kendra began checking into going back to school part-time in the fall. Meanwhile, she continued to work at the Krazie Kutt three days a week. She recognized the fact that it helped her to keep as busy as possible.

Chapter Six

In early August, Dr. Scott requested to speak with Kendra and her father concerning Aimee. She was still in the hospital, but they had been discussing the possibility of hiring a nurse and moving her out to Alfaland.

It was a somber Dr. Scott who greeted them when they walked into his office. Kendra could sense that something wasn't right.

They sat down in the chairs in front of Dr. Scott's desk. Kendra's eyes glanced over at the seascape hanging on the wall. Her memory flashed back for a moment to her last visit and how excited and happy her life was at that moment. "That was two days before our world changed forever," she thought to herself. She crossed her legs and folded her arms across her lap, waiting to hear what Doctor Scott had to say.

"There is just no easy way to tell you this." He rubbed his hands together. "You have all been through so much already, but we have another problem." He hesitated a moment then tilted his head to one side. "Aimee Sue is pregnant."

Kendra and her father stared at the doctor in disbelief.

Kendra broke the silence. "That's not possible, is it?" She shook her head. "I mean, that she could carry it?"

"Well," Dr. Scott replied, "It's not common but it has happened. She was apparently pregnant when the accident happened."

"How can this be?" Mr. Patton stammered. "She wasn't involved with anyone. She didn't even have a boyfriend." He scratched the side of his head.

"Yes, she was involved, Dad," Kendra said, and then added, "and she did have a boyfriend. Just before the tornado hit, she was telling me about this guy, and Dad, she was passionate about him. He was supposed to be coming to visit and meet us all. I kind of forgot about it until now. She never got a chance to tell me his name. I assumed it was someone from college. It is strange, though, when you think about it, why we haven't heard from him. Aimee told me they were deeply in love with each other and she planned to marry him."

"What do we do?" Mr. Patton stared at the doctor for answers. "What will happen to Aimee?" He slid forward on his chair and leaned on the edge of the desk.

"To tell the truth," Dr. Scott admitted, "we are not sure. Aimee's condition is unusual, to say the least. I did call a specialist friend of mine, and he said there have been a few situations similar to this and children have been born. At this point, we find nothing wrong with her except that she's in a coma. She appears to be approximately three and a half months along. Everything relating to that seems to be fine so far."

"How ironic," Kendra thought. "Life is so very strange." She looked at her father. "I can't believe this, can you? Is it ever going to end? Our life has always been so perfect and now everything seems to have fallen apart."

Her father rubbed her shoulder. "I know, it's like we are on a rollercoaster that won't stop. And no, Kendra, it is never going to be the same, but we will make it. It will be good again. We will make it."

"I do have to point out to you that there are some options we could consider," Dr. Scott began to explain.

Mr. Patton lifted his hand, interrupting him. "I don't want to hear that, Jeff. You know me better than that."

"I figured that, but I felt I needed to at least mention it to you. What I suggest is that we continue on for a while and see how she, and the baby, does. There are no signs of permanent brain damage. We'll continue the range of motion and the feeding tube and see what happens. There is still very much the possibility that she will just wake up."

"Dad, I think we should try to locate the father of Aimee's baby."

"Yeah, I agree. He may not be interested, but we need to at least give him that opportunity. I don't understand why we haven't heard from him. It doesn't make any sense. I do concur the man should know, that is, if we can find him."

"I wish she'd have given me his name or where he was from, or something. Maybe if we go through her things we'll find a clue," she suggested. Aimee had brought all her belongings home for the summer and had just thrown most everything in the spare bedroom upstairs. Fortunately for them, the tornado had not affected that room.

"I recall her mentioning several friends," Mr. Patton said, "but very few, if any, last names. I think one was Kathy." He stroked his fingers over his chin. "I think her last name started with an R. Again, it is really strange that he hasn't tried to contact her. I just can't figure this out."

They left the doctor's office and went straight out to Alfaland to search through Aimee's piles of sacks and boxes that she had brought home from school. After nearly an hour had passed, Aunt Jane stood up and placed her hands on her hips.

"There's nothing here that would indicate who she had been involved with or who is the father of her baby," she said. "The only thing is that scribbling." She pointed at a white tablet lying on the floor. At the top of one of her papers in the tablet was written "I Love You" and underneath that, in different handwriting was, "I Love You Too." It was circled with a heart.

"If that is a clue," Byron said rubbing his fingers back and forth over his lower lip. "We don't have anything. I don't know what else to do."

Later in the day, after Kendra had left to go back to work, Mr. Patton contacted the University and they assured him that as soon as classes began they would do some checking around to see if they could find anything, but they really couldn't give him any information at this time.

To their surprise that evening, while Jane and Byron were eating dinner, Kathy Ryan telephoned. She had been Aimee's roommate during her first half of the year at IU and she had stayed on campus to work during the summer. She was sorry to hear what had happened to Aimee and offered her condolences concerning Leigh Patton. She had very little to add to the mystery. Kathy said she knew that Aimee was involved with someone but she'd never met him. She stated that she didn't believe he was a student at the college. She did say that Aimee had left the college on several weekends and didn't return until early Monday morning.

Byron sat back down at the table with Jane and took a sip of coffee. "I'm a little surprised about all this." He looked at Jane. "I thought we could always talk about things as a family. Why didn't Aimee share all this with us?"

"I understand you are a little disappointed," Jane said. "But, sometimes children make a wrong choice. Aimee's human. Maybe this man just swept her off her feet. Perhaps she didn't tell you because she knew you would disapprove. You always said Aimee was a little impulsive, didn't you?"

"Yes, she was. I just don't know what to think. Do you suppose he was just leading her on? It's so difficult watching your children make mistakes. You'd have thought we would have heard from him."

"It could be," Jane said, "that he doesn't know anymore about us then we do him. Maybe that's why he hasn't tried to contact her. It's just difficult to conceive that she wouldn't have given him that information."

Jane stood up and began cleaning off the table.

"I'm so glad you are here Jane." Byron got up to help her. "I don't know how I would have ever made it through all this, if you hadn't have been here."

The following day, Kendra went into the newspaper office to speak with Joey and explain the situation to him. "I've decided I'd rather not enroll in school this fall because of what is going on with Aimee." They discussed it and decided she could spend time at the paper every week and learn the business first hand.

Joey didn't admit it, but he was overjoyed at the prospect because he could spend more time with Kendra. He was coming to the realization that his feelings for Kendra were deeper than just friendship. His emotions were a combination of desire and guilt. He felt like he somehow was cheating on Aaron. In his heart, Joey knew he would never find anyone that could measure up to Kendra. He admired everything about her including the strength that he'd seen in her, which Kendra didn't even realize she had, but he also loved those tender weak moments that she had shared with him.

"She has no idea," Joey thought to himself while Kendra sat by his side at his desk and he explained a few procedures to her. He felt an overwhelming desire to hold her in his arms and tell her how he loved her, but he didn't dare. "Not this soon," he struggled with his thoughts. Joey suppressed his feelings, choosing rather to continue his role as friend and comforter. "At least I can be near her," he concluded. "Besides, perhaps she'd think I am crazy and I could drive her away completely." Thus, Joey continued his pretense.

A few days later on a cloudy and rainy afternoon, he walked by her door and discovered Kendra sitting alone with the lights out in her office. She had her head lying down over her arms.

"Kendra, are you all right?" he asked.

Kendra raised her head and whispered. "Sometimes I get so lonely I don't think I can endure it." She looked into his gentle, compassionate eyes. "Can you please just hold me?"

Joey walked over, took her in his arms, and held her close as he had many times in the last few months. It was like medicine for Kendra when he held her in his arms. She trusted him and knew he understood.

"I feel like you know me better than anyone on earth," she said. Joey's desire overpowered him. He turned his head and kissed her on the lips. Kendra returned his kiss. The two kissed for an endless moment, then, realizing what they were doing, they both stepped back.

"Joey, I'm so sorry. I'm out of control and I'm taking advantage of you. It's so difficult. I miss that love I once had and I get such confused feelings."

"It's not your fault, it's mine. I'm taking advantage of the sorrow that you are going through." He longed to continue holding her. He wanted to pour out his heart to her as she did to him, but his dread of losing her prevented him and he remained silent.

"Please don't let this damage our friendship, Joey," she said. Kendra recognized the fact that Joey had a girlfriend and a life separate from their friendship.

"Nothing will ever destroy our friendship, Kendra," he stated emphatically. "Nothing." He placed his hand on her cheek. "We won't let that happen. Now," he said, "turn your lights on." He flipped the switch on the wall. "And get to work."

Kendra smiled, "Thanks, again, Joey," she said.

"I love that man," she thought to herself. "I wish he were free."

Chapter Seven

The phone was ringing at the Krazie Kutt. It was the last week in October and the leaves were nearly all off of the trees. The weather had turned chilly the last few days and it was obvious that winter was just around the corner. Kendra had been keeping busy working back and forth between the beauty shop and the *Gazette*. She had discovered that keeping busy was the best way to avoid getting depressed. She was proud of all that she had been able to grasp so far about the newspaper business.

"I'll get it," Kendra said. She gave one last finishing touch of spray to the hair of her customer and than ran to answer the phone. She and Carmon tried to take turns getting the phone, which seemed to ring every two minutes.

It was Joey. "I just wanted to let you know," he said, "if you and your family are still concerned about finding the father of Aimee's baby, that there is a private investigator in town. He's going to be here for a few days working on some business for a customer. He works for an agency out of Indianapolis and I understand they are pretty good. Maybe he'd be able to find the mystery man. He's staying at the Ft. Akers Inn and his name is Jared Bradley."

"Thanks, Joey; I think I'm going to try that."

They spoke a few more minutes and then hung up.

They hadn't spoken much since that incident in her office. Joey was being more professional in his dealings with her. "But," Kendra thought, "I care so much for him and I know he's dating someone. I just have to let go. I know one thing, Whoever ends up with Joey will have the best. I just wish things could have been different."

A few minutes later, Kendra phoned Mr. Bradley and made an appointment with him for three that afternoon at the newspaper office.

Three hours later, Jared Bradley stepped into her office and into her life. She was awe struck by how good-looking he was. The denim jacket and black turtleneck emphasized the light blond curly hair that just touched his shoulders and his blue eyes appeared to glow.

"I'm a little surprised," he said. "I expected you to be older, Mrs. Marshall." He put his hand out to shake hers.

"I have to admit I thought the same thing about you, Mr. Bradley." She smiled and took his hand. "Have a seat."

He sat down in a chair in front of her desk. "What is it that you needed to see me about, Mrs. Marshall?"

She told him about Aimee, the coma, and their failed attempts to locate the man with whom she was involved at college. She avoided mentioning the fact of Aimee's pregnancy.

"This doesn't sound too difficult," he said, and advised her of his fee, "If that is suitable?"

"That will not be a problem. Do you need anything in advance?"

"That won't be necessary. Now, I need what information you do have."

"I have it all written down here for you." Kendra handed him a sheet of paper listing all the information that she had collected and felt would be relevant.

Jared Bradley stared at the piece of paper for a considerable length of time without speaking.

"Is there a problem?" Kendra sensed something was bothering him.

He didn't answer.

Kendra tilted her head and said, "Mr. Bradley?"

He hesitated, still looking at the paper, "No, not at all, I was just reading." He folded the paper and placed it in his briefcase. "I'll see what we can come up with. I'll get back with you in a few days. Can you by any chance tell me why you are so desperate to locate this man?"

She decided there was no reason to keep it from him. "I have to admit, I'm a little uneasy about this. Aimee is pregnant, and we feel we should at least let him know what's going on. We realize that he may not want to be found. For all we know he could be a real jerk, and already know and just not care but in reality I don't think Aimee would fall for someone like that. I'm also a little concerned that this may backfire and he may try to take the baby away; if she does have it. That would be so upsetting to us all. Our family has been through so much these last few months."

"I can see that," Jared said, exhibiting a genuine concern in his voice.

They shook hands and he left assuring Kendra, once more, that he would keep in touch.

When he walked out of the office Kendra placed her hand under her chin stroking her fingers up and down across her jaw, thinking. "That has to be the most handsome man I have ever seen, and he is so charming."

Two days passed and Kendra was surprised to run into Jared at the hospital. She walked into Aimee's room and he was standing beside Aimee's bed staring at her. He finally looked up and saw Kendra. "You startled me," he said, "I just wanted to stop by and get a description of your sister. I was going to take a picture of her but she probably looked quite a bit different before this happened. Didn't she?"

"I'm sorry, I didn't think about that." Kendra opened her wallet and pulled out a picture of Aimee. "This is her senior picture." She handed him the picture.

"She was very attractive," he said, taking the picture. "She's so young and innocent." He looked at the picture and then looked back at Aimee. "She looks quite a bit different. Do they have any idea how long she'll be like this?"

"No," Kendra answered. "It could be tomorrow or years from now. They have no idea. Aimee was a bubbly, active, happy person before all this happened. Just minutes before the tornado hit she was so thrilled telling me about how in love she was and that she wanted Aaron and I to meet him as soon as possible."

"That's the last thing she spoke about?" he asked. Jared shook his head. "Aaron? Is that your husband?"

"Yes, he was," Kendra said, her voice cracking. She strained to continue. "He was killed along with my mother in the tornado."

Jared again shook his head in disbelief. "I'm terribly sorry. I understand what you meant the other day when you said your family has been through so much." There was a genuine compassion in his voice and his eyes. He looked into hers and asked. "Where were you and your family when this happened?"

"At Alfaland, that's our family's farm just west of Fort Akers."

"Alfaland, that sounds intriguing. I'd love to see it sometime."

"I'd love to show it to you. I'll be there tomorrow because we are going to move Aimee Sue home, if you'd like to stop out. We've made arrangements with two nurses who will live-in and take turns caring for her. My Aunt Jane will be helping also. We'd have moved her sooner but it isn't easy finding live-in qualified people. Having both ladies there, provides more freedom and neither will be so tied down."

He thought for a moment. "Tomorrow would work. It would have to be after lunch, if that's suitable. I have an appointment for lunch."

"That would be fine." Kendra took a note pad off of Aimee's dresser and wrote down the directions and gave to him.

"We'll see you tomorrow then," he said. He turned and walked out the door.

Kendra was impressed with him. "I feel as if he's a friend even though I've just met him," she thought. She was looking forward to showing him Alfaland tomorrow.

Chapter Eight

It was getting late and Jane was exhausted from her full day of preparing for Aimee's return home tomorrow and the addition of the two nurses, Sarah and Judy. She loved taking care of things at Alfaland, but she was beginning to feel a slight bit uncomfortable. It wasn't that she didn't love being at Alfaland. It was just the opposite. She loved it too much. The last three months had been the first time in her life that she had felt really needed. She'd had a good life and had seen much of the world, but always alone. Her school children had been her whole life. Now all that had changed.

She had spent hours talking with and consoling with Byron. She knew how much he had loved her sister, Leigh. Now she was falling in love with this brilliant man and didn't know how to deal with it. Jane washed her face and brushed her teeth. "I can't let things go on this way," she thought, "but every time I suggest leaving, Byron asks me to please stay a little longer. I know he needs me but it isn't appropriate, my staying on like this."

She finished brushing her teeth and walked over to her bed and sat down.

"This is so difficult," she thought. Jane had never been married, and her desire for a man and for love was immense. "I have to move out. I don't have any other choice." She slipped off her watch and laid it on the night stand. "I'll leave tomorrow once Aimee is moved back home. That settles it." She crawled into bed for the night struggling to hold back the tears that were endeavoring to stream down her cheeks.

Byron Patton lay quietly in his big empty bed at Alfaland. So much had changed in his life. He couldn't sleep, as usual. All he could do was think. Every night his mind went back over the dreadful day that took his lovely wife of twenty-eight years. Leigh, he loved and missed her so. He stroked his hand over her side of the bed. He remembered the years past, the birth of their two lovely daughters and the love and joy that they all had shared. It was gone. Over.

He had also been struggling for days with feelings for Jane. She had given him the encouragement he needed to go on. Now he found himself having desires for her that troubled him. "Oh God, Leigh, what am I doing?" he thought. "I'm sorry. I'm just so lonely and she's so special to me. She's here and you're not." He felt guilty. He lay in his bed, struggling within himself and praying. "Oh God, what's wrong with me? Why do I have these feelings for Jane?"

He was lonely and she was there, in the bedroom upstairs. She'd been suggesting leaving for the last couple of weeks and he kept begging her to stay. Why? He knew the truth, but he was having a hard time facing it. He was falling in love with Jane, and he felt guilty about it.

He found himself slipping out of his bed in the middle of the night and walking toward Jane's room. They were alone in the house. Tomorrow they would be bringing Aimee home and Sarah and Judy would be moving in. He knew Jane was going to leave and he didn't want that to happen. He had to talk to her! He stood silently in her doorway.

"Byron? Is that you?" Jane's soft voice called out. "Would you like to come in?"

"Jane, I'm sorry. I guess I have put too much on you. On us both."

"I know, its okay, I understand. I need you too," she said. "Come here and sit down. Let's talk about it." She sat up and leaned her back against the headboard.

"I feel so guilty," he said.

"This is difficult for me too."

He walked over and sat on the bed with Jane. Without saying a word, he took her in his arms and held her close as they cried. They needed each other so. Leigh was gone and they were falling in love. It seemed so right.

"Jane?" He asked while holding her close. "Will you please stay? I don't mean for a while, I mean forever. I don't want to go on alone and I don't want to go on with anyone else. I'm lonely, but when I'm with you I'm happy and content. I have no desire to look for anyone else."

"What about Kendra and your parents or the neighbors. They may not understand."

"Let's just keep our feelings a secret for a little while longer," he said. "And then, when we both agree that the time is right, we'll announce we are getting married. That is if you would. Will you marry me, Jane?"

"Oh, Byron, I've needed love for so long. I never dreamed I'd find someone like you. You know and I know, and Leigh knows, if she can hear, that I'd never have come between you and her." She placed her fingers on his cheek. "I do love you so. I've been falling in love with you for weeks now. I believe too that we should get married. Yes, I'll stay. I'll stay by your side for the rest of my life. Somehow, I feel that's the way it was meant to be, but I agree we should wait to tell anyone for a while. At least things will be less inappropriate tomorrow after everyone else moves in."

"Maybe sometime between Thanksgiving and Christmas," Byron suggested. "As difficult as it will be, we can sleep in separate beds until then. I think what we share is worth waiting for."

"Tonight will be our secret." She kissed him on the lips. Jane too was having mixed feelings. Joy was over pouring in her heart. She had never loved a man so deeply, but, along with it, she had feelings of guilt. "This will give us some time to work things out," she said.

It took every ounce of strength that he had to lift himself up and pull away from her. "This will be worth waiting for," he said as he left the room.

Jane was glad he had the strength to leave because she didn't believe she could have. She loved and admired him for it.

The ambulance transported Aimee Sue back home to Alfaland the following morning. It was quite an ordeal to set up the feeding tube equipment and everything else that Aimee needed. The nurses, Judy and Sarah, sisters and both widows in their sixties, were highly recommended and qualified.

With her usual warmth and charm Jane had prepared Aimee's old room for her.

"I'm impressed. This is so cheery, Jane. You are so good to us," Kendra said, following her into Aimee's room. Kendra looked around the room and then at Jane. "I don't know how we'd have survived without you." She walked over and embraced her.

Seeing Aimee lying there in her own bedroom turned out to be an emotional moment for them all. Aimee appeared to be in a normal sleep except her face which appeared thin and lifeless. Kendra had made it a point to keep Aimee's hair neat and styled for her.

"She looks like Sleeping Beauty," Jane said. She stood over Aimee and stroked her forehead.

"It's good to have her home," Byron said, "Where she belongs."

Sarah and Judy were going to share Kendra's old bedroom, which had an adjoining door to Aimee's room. This would be much easier for all of them. No more running to the hospital.

Jared Bradley drove his white Jeep Cherokee up the lengthy drive to Alfaland shortly after one o'clock. Kendra spotted him coming and went outside to meet him.

Jared smiled as he surveyed the property with his eyes. "This is nice, really nice." His eyes fixed on one large pine tree in the center of the yard that was missing the top half.

Kendra saw him eyeing it. "That is about the only physical evidence of the tornado that is left," she said.

Kendra escorted him inside to the kitchen and introduced him to her father and Jane.

Jared shook Byron's hand. "I'm so pleased to meet you and I'm very sorry about the tragedy you and your family have endured. It's hard to conceive how life can be altered forever in one minute. You all have been through so much."

"I appreciate that," Byron said. "Kendra tells me that you are going to be looking for our mystery man. I admit I have mixed feelings where this man is concerned. A part of me would like to punch him in the nose, but on the other hand, I realize that Aimee must have loved him very much, and besides that, he is the father of my grandchild."

"That's a natural way for a father who loves his daughter to feel, Mr. Patton," Jared said. "I'll see what I can do."

"Come on, I'll show you around," Kendra said, taking his hand and escorting him through the entire house, including Aimee's room, where she introduced him to Sarah and Judy.

"Nice to meet you, ladies," he said and shook their hands.

She finished at the room on the third floor, where they lingered for some time at the back double windows overlooking Alfaland. "Right now, this is being used mainly for storage as you can see." There were a few boxes and odd pieces of furniture sitting around. "This was my and Aimee's hide out when we were kids. We played up here a lot. I always loved this room." She leaned against the window frame. "Sometimes at night," Kendra said, "Mom and Dad didn't know this, but we'd sneak out of bed and come up here, open the window and crawl out on the roof. We'd set and look at the stars for hours."

"I bet it was beautiful. It's beautiful now," Jared said. "You and your sister have so many good memories. I sometimes wish I'd have had a brother or sister to grow up with. I was an only child. "I'm sure living in the country has its advantages." He laid his arms against the window ledge and looked out. "I've always lived in the city, South Bend and now Indianapolis."

They made their way back downstairs and out to the screened

front porch, which spanned the entire length of the house. It was filled with two porch swings, several wooden chairs, plants and a table, which Mr. Patton had made. In the center was a large ping-pong table.

"Would you like something to drink before I give you the outside tour? Kendra asked.

"Coffee sounds great." He smiled at her, "With two sugars."

Kendra enjoyed seeing him smile. "He has a lovely smile," she thought.

Kendra left and returned moments later carrying a tray with their coffee and a verity of homemade cookies that Jane had made.

"This has got to be the loveliest place I have ever seen," Jared said. He stood admiring the view from the south side of the porch overlooking the orchard. "Look." He pointed. "At those three squirrels racing around that tree." He glanced toward her and smiled.

"It is lovely," Kendra said. "Sometimes we have deer come right up next to the house along with the rabbits, raccoons, and opossum. You name it," she chuckled, "even skunks."

"You talk as if you still live here," he said.

"No, I'm staying at our apartment in town. I love it here but," she hesitated a moment. "To tell you the truth, I feel lonely when I'm here too long. Does that make any sense?"

"I guess I can see that," he said, "sort of like having a vacation alone. Even if it is beautiful it's just not the same if you don't have someone to share it with." He took the tray from her hands. "Here let me help you with that."

They sat down at the round wooden table in the corner of the porch, and Jared placed the cookies between them. The view to the east overlooked the drive to the road, the pasture and the fields beyond. An assortment of birds were pecking and tossing seed from a feeder Mr. Patton had placed outside the porch.

"I feel like," he hesitated, reflecting for a moment, "like I'm in another world. I bet it was interesting growing up here." He reached for a peanut butter cookie and took a large bite.

"I couldn't have asked for a better childhood. I love it here. A part of me is here. It always will be."

"I admire your enthusiasm when you share about your childhood." He grinned. "I can envision you as a tall, skinny little girl with freckles and pigtails running through the fields."

Kendra laughed.

"These cookies are good." He reached for another one. "Did you make them?"

She shook her head, "No," my aunt did. She's always baking something delicious. "I love the chocolate chip ones." She reached and took one off the tray.

They sat at the table and talked for nearly an hour before pouring themselves another cup of coffee, grabbing a couple more cookies, and exiting through the front screen door to the outside. Kendra guided him through the orchard and around to the back yard to the swimming pool. It was a warm and sunny day for the end of October and there were several piles of leaves scattered throughout the property that hadn't yet been picked up.

"It's quite an ordeal raking here in the fall, even using the tractor," Kendra said.

Jared looked around. "I can imagine."

They came to a stop on the cement patio by the pool.

"This is where Aimee was found."

Jared's voice became somber. "In the pool?" he asked.

Kendra nodded.

He shook his head. "It's tragic."

Making their way down to the pond, Kendra was surprised when she noticed that the footbridge had been rebuilt. Her father hadn't mentioned it.

Looking over at Jared she said, "It's remarkable how all the neighbors have pitched in and rebuilt everything. Over there on the footbridge is where my husband was when the tornado hit. That was the last time I saw him. He was standing on the bridge and he waved at me. They found him the next day in the water." She turned her head away. She could still picture him standing there.

"I'm sorry," Jared said. "If this is too difficult for you…"

"No, I'm fine." She smiled and motioned, "Come on, I'll show you the horses."

They walked leisurely back up the hill and toward the barn.

Buster had cornered a couple of cats under a woodpile behind the barn. Kendra shouted, "Buster, get away from there!" Buster halted his amusement and ran to her. He stayed but a second and then ran back toward the house. She laughed. "He loves it out here."

Jared waved his hands in the air. "Lots of space for him to run," he said.

"I like being with this man," Kendra admitted to herself. She was experiencing some emotions that surprised her.

Kendra escorted him to the stables and walked up to the stall of her favorite horse. She placed her arms around the horse's neck. "This is Patience. Isn't she a beauty?" she asked. "She's my girl." Kendra patted the horse on the neck.

He smiled in agreement. "She is." He was thinking what a beautiful woman Kendra was.

"Thank goodness the barn was not hit by the tornado." Kendra rubbed the horse on the top of her head between the ears. "As far as we know none of the animals were affected." She looked at Jared. "I have an idea," she said. "Would you like to go riding?"

"I'd love to," Jared said, "but, it's been quite a while since I've been on a horse!" He was cautious. "Are they pretty gentle horses? Will you promise not to laugh?"

Kendra lifted her hand, as if to swear, "I promise not to laugh."

George, Mr. Patton's hired hand, was nearby and helped her saddle up the horses. She gave Patience to Jared, since she was the most gentle, and Kendra rode Aimee Sue's horse, Jenny.

Kendra looked over at Jared and smiled. "It feels terrific to be ridding again. I haven't ridden for several months." They walked the horses side by side down the hill, around the pond, and then entered the path that went through the woods.

Jared looked over at her and sighed. "I haven't ridden in years." He stroked the horse on the neck.

Kendra grinned at him. "You look like a character in a TV western."

"I hope that's a compliment," he said.

"It is," she said.

She proceeded to show him some remains of the forts that she Aimee and the neighborhood kids had built years before. "I can't believe any of this is still intact," Kendra said. She laughed and pointed out a carving that they had put on a tree "Bar P Ranch". "That stands for Bar Patton Ranch." She laughed. "That was the name we gave this place."

"Sounds like an interesting childhood," Jared said.

They nudged the horses and continued on through the woods.

They stopped and got off the horses at an old bridge, east at the edge of the woods.

"This bridge is about shattered." Kendra said.

Jared walked over and looked under the bridge. "I don't think I'd want to walk over this."

"It doesn't get used anymore." Kendra said. She sat down on the fallen trunk of a tree. "That's probably why Daddy didn't repair it. He used it for the cattle when we had them."

Jared sat down beside her. They sat for several minutes studying the view overlooking the property.

"This would make an incredible picture," Jared said. "It looks like you can see the whole property from here. The house and the barn look so far away."

"I use to hang out here a lot when I was young." Kendra shared with him. She looked toward the house off in the distance. "I'd come here when I was upset about something and sit here on the bridge. It was my quiet spot in the world where I'd sort things out or pout or whatever." She laughed and looked at Jared. "I'm sorry. I'm pouring out all this childhood stuff on you."

"I'm enjoying it." Jared looked at her and smiled. "You sure couldn't ask for a better spot then this." He leaned toward her and jested, "To pout."

They both laughed.

Getting back on the horses, they continued on through the woods to the south edge of the farm which came out on Patton Road.

Kendra stopped her horse. She looked at Jared grinning into his blue eyes. "Do you want to go for it?"

It took a moment until he realized what she meant. "I'm game if you are." He agreed, grinning and nodding back at her. "Let's go for it!"

They nudged the horses and began to race at a full gallop down the road. The horse's hooves pounded the gravel road beneath them and their leather saddles squeaked with each lunge forward. They raced around the curve in the road and passed the pasture to the drive. The horses began to pant but they were enjoying the run. They stayed neck and neck until they reached the drive when Kendra pulled ahead.

It took considerable effort for her to get Jenny to stop before she ran full speed into the barn.

Jared was out of breath himself. "Now that was fun. I'll probably be bow legged tomorrow morning." He stood in the stirrup, threw his leg over the horse, and jumped to the ground. "I haven't had so much fun in a long time."

Kendra was happy that he enjoyed himself.

George took the horses for them. Kendra and Jared turned toward his Jeep and, like a magnet their hands came together as they walked to his vehicle. Jared appeared somber when he got into the Jeep.

"Thanks for a wonderful afternoon," he said. He looked into her eyes. "You may not believe it but, this is the best time I've had in a very long time."

"Me too," she said. Kendra hated to see him leave.

"I'll be heading for Indy tonight. I'll get back with you soon." He closed the door.

Kendra put her hands on the window frame of his Jeep. "Thank you," she said.

Their eyes met for a cherished instant that was filled with a multitude of unspoken words.

Kendra stood, with a heavy heart, and watched him as he drove off. She watched until he was out of sight.

Chapter Nine

On Friday, the beauty shop was buzzing with activity. Chattering voices filled the room from every direction. Kendra and Carmon both had several appointments. The new tanning bed had been running since six o'clock that morning.

Shortly before noon, much to Kendra's surprise, Jared Bradley walked into the shop looking for her. He was more handsome than she had remembered. Kendra felt something ignite inside her when she saw him. She could sense her face burning and her heart pounding.

Kendra made a feeble attempt to appear casual, as she walked over to the counter to speak to him. "Hi, I've been wondering how things were going. So, did you find him?" She hoped he didn't notice her excitement at his presence. She was thankful, she'd been in the tanning bed the last couple of days and her face was a combination of red and freckles because of it.

"Would you have time to go to lunch?" He appeared to be a little uptight and serious.

"Sure, give me about five minutes."

"Okay, I'll wait for you outside," he said and went back out the door. "What is the matter with me; why am I so tense?" he questioned himself. He leaned his back against the Jeep and crossed his arms. "I have got to be crazy."

After Jared's exit, Kendra grabbed her purse, sprayed on a little cologne and, with shaky fingers, applied some lip-gloss and eye shadow.

Carmon, who was in the process of cutting a patron's hair, stared at her in amazement. She'd never seen Kendra like this. "That's quite a hunk you've got there."

"It's nothing," Kendra said. "He's just the private investigator we hired."

"I see." Carmon nodded and grinned.

Kendra met Jared in the parking lot and they walked to a bakery-cafe on East Market Street near the beauty shop.

Jared began after they each had ordered a chicken salad sandwich and soup. "I have to confess that this was not as easy as I thought it would be." He took a sip of his cola. "I'm afraid I've come up with nothing," he said, "Zero." The one possibility that I have considered is that he could have been a foreign student and he went back home. There is another thing I was wondering about. Did Aimee bring her belongings home from college, and if so, could I look through them? Maybe there would be a clue somewhere that would help me."

"It wouldn't be a problem if you want to look through her things but we did do that." She lifted the spoon to her mouth, took a sip of soup, paused for a moment, and then continued. "But we may have missed something. Would you want to do it tomorrow?"

"That would suit me fine." He swallowed a bite of his sandwich and then said, "I want to visit my mother this weekend anyway, since I didn't get to see her the last time I was here."

"Where does your mother live?" Kendra took a bite of her sandwich.

"She lives in South Bend and I'm anxious to give her the good news. He paused a moment and swallowed. "I am really excided about this! Our agency wants me to open up a new branch office in South Bend. So I'll be closer. She'll be happy about that. My mother is a dear." He shook his head and grinned. "She's so involved with everything, especially her art. She has a small studio and teaches several students."

Kendra detected how he was beginning to loosen up. She wanted to know everything about him. "That's fascinating! How did you get into the private investigator business, and to live in Indianapolis?"

He took another sip and put down his drink. "My father was a detective for the South Bend Police Department before he was killed during a drug operation. I have always been interested in law enforcement so after high school I went to Vincennes University for two years majoring in law enforcement. But after school, I had a difficult time finding a job. A friend of mine from school told me about this position and I checked it out, got the job, and here I am. I've learned a lot and they say I do a good job. I get to travel quite a bit, and I enjoy that. I'm really keyed up about opening up this branch office. I'll be twenty-seven next month and I'm ready to set a little direction in my life. I'd still like to become a police officer sometime, though." He leaned his elbows on the table and gestured toward her with his hands. "Okay, enough about me, what about you?"

She swallowed, and then wiped her mouth with her napkin. "All my plans are in disarray after this year. When I married Aaron last year, I thought the direction for my life was set, and then everything happened. It amazes me how one day can so totally change a person's life. December was when our baby was to be born." Her face became serious. "I lost my baby when I fell down the steps during the tornado. She sighed but then smiled, "Now, I'm waiting to see what happens with Aimee and working part time at the beauty shop and the *Fort Akers Gazette*, where we first met. I inherited the paper when my husband died so Joey, he's the manager, is attempting to teach me the business."

Jared slipped his arm over the center of the table and wrapped his fingers around her wrist. "I'm sorry." His voice was filled with compassion. "Your husband was apparently a very special person."

Jared felt overwhelmingly drawn to this lovely lady. He loved being with her. He pulled back his hand.

After hesitating a moment he asked, "Are you free tonight? Why not go with me to see Mother? You'll like her and I know she'll be fond of you. It'll do her good to see me with someone." He laughed, "She's always concerned, that I don't have any social life."

"I guess so. I don't have any plans for tonight. I'd love to. I won't be free until about four, if you want to pick me up at my apartment."

Jared walked her back to the beauty shop after they had finished their lunch. "I'll pick you up about four thirty, and afterwards we'll stop for dinner somewhere."

Jared felt an excitement in his life that he hadn't felt for sometime. "Maybe somehow this could all work," he thought to himself. But then another side said, "Why, does life have to be so damn complicated?" He pounded the steering wheel with the palm of his hand. Things were different now. He'd met Kendra, the most beautiful and fascinating women he'd ever known. Why couldn't he have met her earlier in his life? How could he ever tell her about the past? "I can't; I won't." He refused to think about it. He wasn't going to let pain infiltrate this lovely day. He'd deal with that later. "I'll think of something. I'll think about it later."

Jared was correct. Kendra did like Lori Bradley. It was obvious from where Jared had received his good looks. Lori was a beautiful woman. She looked like a teenager in the huge blue and yellow plaid flannel shirt she was wearing. Only in her face was it revealed that she was in her forties. It was evident that she was proud and fond of her only child. She showed them around her studio. Kendra was impressed with Lori's artwork, especially one remarkable oil canvas of a stunning wild horse standing on a mountain in the moonlight. Kendra was awed by it.

Lori brewed some honey and lemon tea for them. "Would you both like something to eat? I already had a bite to eat. If I'd have known you were coming I'd have prepared something."

"I'm sorry mom, I should have called." Jared apologized. "Thanks for the offer but we are planning to stop somewhere and eat."

Lori's apartment, above the studio was a cozy place with lots of trinkets, woodcarvings and figurines sitting everywhere. A picture of a handsome man in a police uniform was on the coffee table. Kendra assumed that this was Jared's father.

They had a lovely time. The two women did most of the talking while Jared listened. Kendra regretted when they had to leave. Lori Bradley was one of these people who possessed an enthusiasm for life that drew those around her into it.

"Your mother is a very special person," Kendra commented during the drive back to Fort Akers. "I enjoyed her very much."

"I knew you'd like her." Jared smiled.

"Why don't we go to my place and I'll fix spaghetti." Kendra suggested. "If you like spaghetti, and garlic bread?"

"I love spaghetti. That's a terrific idea."

"I have a roommate that you haven't met," she smiled.

Jared looked a little surprised. He didn't say anything, but he was curious.

Buster gave them his usual greeting at the door.

"This is my buddy and roommate," Kendra said. She leaned over and gave Buster a hug and pat on the back.

Jared rolled his eyes. "I see you have a sense of humor too, don't you?"

They laughed.

"Have a seat." Kendra pointed toward her leather chair and ottoman. "I'll go and get dinner started. The TV controller is there on the ottoman, if you like."

Jared and Buster quickly made friends. "What can I do?" he shouted to Kendra who had gone to the kitchen.

"Would you like to throw together a salad? You can do that if you like."

He walked into the kitchen. "I like." He helped create a salad out of whatever he could find and sliced the garlic bread while Kendra made the spaghetti.

"It's nice," Kendra said to him when they sat down to eat.

"What's that?" He smiled.

"To have someone here." She reached for the ranch dressing and poured it over her salad, then handed the dressing to him. "This place has been so lonely. I'm glad you appeared in my life, Mr. Bradley. It's hard. I mean, being lonely. I never in my life experienced it till this year. I guess I've been fortunate." She took a slice of garlic bread and handed the plate to him. "I've also been fortunate to have Joey, and Carmon, who have helped me so much through all this. You met Joey at the newspaper office. I think the world of that man. But, he's got his own life. I can't keep depending on him like I have."

"I'm glad I met you, too." He smiled at her. "I love your honesty and ability to share your feelings." He took a slice of bread and sat the plate back on the table. "It's not that easy for me." He twisted his fork in his spaghetti, then paused and looked at her before taking a bite. "This has been a lonely year for me, too."

"You've lost someone too, haven't you, Jared?" she asked.

"Is it that obvious?" He looked down at his fork.

"What happened?"

He wiped his hands with his napkin, leaned back in his chair, and then stared at her for a moment. "It's somewhat painful for me." He said, unsure of what or how much he wanted to say. "But, let's just say that she left me." He took a sip of his drink and set it back on the table. "To tell you the truth, I'd rather concentrate on now and the future. I can't change the past, but I can change the future, and, I plan to." He laid his hands on the table. His eyes lit up and a broad smile appeared on his face. "Do you know, Kendra Marshall, that you are a very, very beautiful lady?"

Kendra smiled. "I can see you don't want to dwell on the past. Neither do I." She wiped her mouth with her napkin and then took a sip of her drink. "You can get weary of being sad all the time." She got up, reaching for his plate to get him more spaghetti. "Do you know what I mean?" She asked. She took his plate and refilled it from the pan on the stove.

"Yes, I really do." He reached and took his plate from her hand. "Sometimes we just have to let go or the past will destroy us," he said.

Kendra was curious as to what he meant. "What had happened in his life that was so devastating?" she thought.

Jared helped her tidy the kitchen after dinner.

"I can see you've had experienced at this." Kendra laughed. "So how are you at cooking?"

"I love to cook." He dried a plate and placed it in the cupboard. "My specialty is Chinese food. Do you like Chinese food?" he asked.

"I sure do!" she said.

"Once I get my apartment, I'll prepare you one of my scrumptious Chinese dinners. I've been thinking about getting an apartment here in Fort Akers." He folded his towel and hung it over the sink. "I like this community and it is close to South Bend."

"I'd like that," Kendra said, looking into his beautiful blue eyes. "I'd like that very much."

Unable to restrain himself any longer, Jared took the glass she was drying and put it in the cabinet. He then leaned against the counter, took hold of her hands and pulled her to him. Their lips merged as one. They continued to kiss, each saturated with a hunger and desire for love that was overpowering to them.

"I am so glad I met you," he said. "I never thought I could be interested in anyone again, but you've brought me back to life." He stroked the side of her face. "I felt drawn to you from the first moment that I saw you that afternoon in the newspaper office."

"That's exactly how I felt," she said. "I was attracted to you that first day, too." She stepped back and took his hands in hers. "Please be patient with me," she asked. Her voice and expression grew serious, "I'm going through some crazy emotions right now. I can't seem to shake this feeling that I am cheating on Aaron." She looked up into his eyes. "Can you understand?"

He nodded, "Yes, I do understand." He placed his thumb under her chin and stroked her cheek with his fingers. "We'll take it slow. I don't want to lose what I've found in you, Kendra."

Their lips met again.

Sensing a fresh joy and excitement coming alive within her, Kendra nestled in Jared's arms on the sofa and they watched a classic

Frankenstein movie that was on television. Near the end of the movie Jared turned and caressed Kendra's cheek with the back of his hand. He brushed her hair back behind her ear with his fingertips. He then placed his hand on the back of her head and pulled her to him and kissed her again and again.

Kendra's insides sparked with an uncontrollable desire that she hadn't felt for some time. "I'm shocked," she thought, "that I could feel like this so soon after Aaron's death." A war between wild desire and disappointment burned inside her.

Jared's passion continued to mount; he, with shaky fingers, pushed her hair back and began kissing around her neck and ear. He, at that moment, remembered what she had just said about taking it slow. Jared pulled back and stared into her eyes. "I think I should probably get going," he said.

Kendra kissed the top of his hand. "I hate for you to leave, but I'm also relieved," she said. "I'm not ready for anything more. Where are you going?"

"Back to the motel; I've rented a room there for the weekend."

Arm in arm, they walked to the door where they embraced one last time, each sensing a new hope in their heart.

They both went to their separate beds, but something was different now. Neither was feeling that deep sense of loss that had engulfed them for the last six months.

The phone ringing awakened Kendra at nine o'clock the following morning. It was Jared.

"Hi, you look beautiful this morning," Jared said.

Kendra laughed. "Thank you. So do you." She sat up in bed. Hearing his voice warmed her heart. "You know, I slept better than I have in months."

"So did I!" he said. He lied. The truth was he had tossed and turned all night. "My mother really likes you," he said.

"You spoke to your mother already this morning?" she asked.

"Yes, I was so wound up when I woke up, and I didn't want to wake you at seven o'clock, so I woke her."

"The feeling is mutual, I really liked her too," Kendra said.

"I'm afraid I have some bad news," Jared said. "At least, I feel its bad news. My boss called me this morning. I am going to have to go to California for a couple of weeks. He wants me to finish up a case we are working on before I move back to South Bend. Our client is in a hurry, and I'm the only one available to go. He has a court date in three weeks, and we need to track down some information for him."

There was no hiding her disappointment. They were just getting to know each other. She liked being with him.

"Would you like some breakfast?" he asked.

"I'd love it."

"How would you like for me to bring it to you?"

"Fantastic, but I need a little time!" Kendra twisted the phone cord around her little finger. She felt like a kid again. "You're going to spoil me."

"You deserve it. I'll be there in a half hour and I'll bring Buster something, too."

Kendra sang along with the music while in the shower. She had turned the volume up extra loud, so she could hear it. "It's so wonderful to feel something again!" she thought. She slipped into a pair of jeans and a sweatshirt and then let Buster out.

They embraced and kissed when Jared arrived.

"It is so pleasant to have a man's arms around me again," Kendra thought to herself.

"I hope food from McDonalds restaurant is okay." He sat the sack on the kitchen table and began emptying the breakfast sandwiches and juice. "Can Buster have sausage?" he asked.

"I suppose. You're spoiling us." Kendra grinned. She got a couple of plates out of the cabinet for them to use.

"I'm no dummy." Jared squatted down to the dog's level and broke up a piece of sausage into Buster's bowl. "I have to get past the dog to get close to his master." He raised and lowered his eyebrows several times.

Kendra laughed.

After breakfast, they put Buster in the back seat of the jeep and drove out to Alfaland so Jared could go through Aimee's things to see if he could find any new information.

Kendra sat on the floor with her legs crossed and watched Jared as he went through the boxes of books and papers Aimee had brought home from school.

Jared found a couple of phone numbers in a tablet and tore them out. "I'll check these out. They may be something." He looked at Kendra. "Did Aimee have a checkbook?"

"Yes, it's in here." Kendra opened a dresser drawer, found Aimee's checkbook, and then handed it to him. "I never even thought of that. Dad's closed it out."

"Do you mind if I take this? There may be some clues where she wrote checks."

"Sure, go ahead. She won't be using that one anymore. She only had that account for college."

Jared found a couple of pictures that he kept, but Kendra didn't recognize any of the people in them.

After spending over an hour going through Aimee's things, Kendra and Jared joined Jane and Byron who were on the porch taking a coffee break from the strenuous job of raking leaves.

Mr. Patton pushed his foot, causing the swing he was sitting on to begin swinging back and forth. "Did you find anything useful, Jared?" he asked.

"I don't think so. There's not much to go on," Jared said. "Did Kendra mention my theory that he may have been a foreign student?"

"Yes, she did." He rubbed his fingers across his chin. "That's a possibility." He shook his head and sighed, "I sure wish Aimee would have told us what was going on."

After Kendra and Jared had left, Jane looked at Byron and asked, "What do you think?"

"I think Kendra is crazy about this fellow," he said.

"That's what I was noticing," Jane said. "How do you feel about that?"

"It's fast, but I know how hurt and lonely she's been. I sure can't say anything, can I?" He smiled and threw her a kiss. "All I want is for her to be happy. The only thing is, you and I have known each other for a long time. She just met this fellow. I'll be honest; there is something about Jared that makes me a little uneasy. I can't say what, but it does." He pushed his foot and began swinging again. "The truth is I was hoping her and Joey Dubois would get together sometime. He's such a nice person. It is so difficult watching the girls' lives playing out before me and not being able to intervene. I can't help Aimee at all, and I don't know what I'd say to Kendra."

"Well, love," he said, "I guess break is over. We'll never get done if we don't quit taking breaks." Jane picked up her yellow sock cap and pulled it down over her ears and zipped up her hooded sweatshirt. They headed back outside to continue their work in the yard.

"I think Sarah and Judy are on to us," Jane said grinning as they headed around to the back of the house to pick up where they had left off.

"I think so too. I believe it's time we set a date and make the announcement. Besides, lovely lady, I don't think I can hold out much longer. You're driving me crazy. I'd love nothing more than to throw you down in these leaves and make mad and passionate love to you."

Jane chuckled, "As many leaves as we have piled here, we could probably disappear in them." She smiled and looked into his eyes. "I can tell my life is going to be interesting married to you, Mr. Patton."

"I love you, Jane." He felt awkward saying it.

"I love you too, Byron. I agree the time is right."

It was nearing one o'clock by the time Kendra and Jared arrived back at her apartment.

"I wish you didn't have to leave," Kendra said.

He smiled and touched her cheek. "When I get done with this, I'll be back and you won't be able to get rid of me. I could use your help finding an apartment and setting up my business, if you would be interested. You can keep your eyes open for me. I may even consider renting or buying a house instead of an apartment."

She wrapped her arms around his slender waist. "How soon do you have to go?"

"My plane leaves out of Indianapolis at seven tonight, so I'll have to be leaving shortly. If it's okay, I'll call you?"

"You better," she said.

"I have something for you before I go," he said. Jared ran out to his Jeep and came back with a plastic bag. He pulled out a fuzzy stuffed teddy bear and gave it to her. "This is for you to cuddle while I'm gone. His name is Jared, also." He grinned. "Now, you'll notice that he has a watch around his paw. When the alarm on that watch goes off, you'll know that I'm on my way home. We don't want you to get lonely, so whenever you do, just cuddle little fuzzy here, okay?"

Moved by his sweet gesture, Kendra smiled. "I've never met anyone like you, Jared." She hugged him, squashing the teddy bear in between them.

He looked at her, his eyes sparkled. "That's also so you won't forget me, my sweet."

"I don't think so," she said. "I don't think you have to worry about that."

They shared several prolonged passion filled kisses before Kendra walked with Jared to his Jeep.

Kendra stood for several moments after Jared had left, holding the fuzzy gray teddy bear in her arms and then turned to walk back to her apartment. She realized something special was happening. She wasn't feeling the emptiness that she had felt. She didn't feel alone. She had something to look forward to, a new hope in her heart.

For every minute of every mile that elapsed during the trip to Indianapolis, Jared's thoughts were besieged with Kendra. He hoped nothing would change while he was gone.

Chapter Ten

The next few weeks, in spite of Jared being gone, a new hope arose in Kendra's heart and mind. Jared phoned her often, mostly late at night. They would talk at times for more than an hour. Things were going fine for Jared, but he discovered after the second week that he wasn't going to make it back until at least the weekend after Thanksgiving. He had turned over the information concerning Aimee to his boss to work on while he was gone. Kendra was disappointed that Jared couldn't be there for the Thanksgiving holiday. Even though, so far, she had refrained from mentioning her newfound relationship with Jared to anyone because she wasn't sure how people would respond, especially her father.

Kendra was spending more and more of her time becoming educated about the newspaper business. She was gaining confidence and beginning to tackle some difficult jobs. The crew that worked at the paper had been fond of Aaron and showed her their affection and respect because of it.

Joey was making a conscious effort to back off, for the time being, as far as Kendra was concerned. He wanted to give her the time that he was convinced she needed, but his love for her continued to grow stronger each day.

Thanksgiving Day at Alfaland was a day of joy and sentiment. Aunt Jane had invited Joey and Carmon to join them for dinner since both of their families lived far away. Kendra had picked Carmon up early and they went out to Alfaland to help prepare the dinner. Jane gave them the choice jobs of making the stuffing and a toss salad.

Kendra leaned over and put her arm around Jane, "Jane I hope we have lots of sage; Daddy likes lots of sage in his dressing."

"I know," Jane said, "he already informed me of that. Why do you think I'm letting you two make it?"

"Here I thought it was because you were fond of our cooking." Kendra grinned.

Joey appeared at the door at twelve-thirty with two pumpkin pies, a container of whipping cream, and his guitar, which Jane had informed him, was a requirement for dinner.

"I want you to know I did not buy these pies. These are home made pies, although they don't look like grandmas." He laughed. "You'll be able to tell by the crusts. I've been up since six o'clock working on them. Would you believe I had to throw out two crusts before I created these? Pie crusts are not easy. You should see my kitchen."

"Joey, they look great," Kendra said. "I can't believe you did this. I usually use the pre-made crusts. I'm impressed." Kendra gave him a warm hug and Carmon took his coat.

"They look fantastic to me," Carmon said, "better than any I've ever made."

Joey put his guitar in the corner of the room and went in to sit down with Mr. Patton in the living room where there was a fire burning in the fireplace.

"Fire feels great," Joey said. "It's getting cold out there." He rubbed his hands together. "And it's just beginning to spit a little snow."

"How is Kendra's training going at the paper?" Byron asked. He was still hoping in the back of his mind that Joey and Kendra would get together sometime.

"She's doing great. She's got what it takes," Joey said. "You can be proud of her."

The women, which included Sarah and Judy, completed their work in the kitchen and then joined Joey and Byron in the living room. Jane walked over and stood in front of the fireplace. "Your father has set up our dinner table in Aimee's room," Jane said. "So what we are going to do is fix our plates and carry them up stairs and eat our Thanksgiving dinner with Aimee."

Kendra walked over and kissed her father on the cheek. "Only you could come up with something like this."

The small group lined up in the kitchen, filled their plates, and then carried them up the stairs to Aimee's room.

Once they were all seated around the table, they held hands and Byron prayed, giving thanks for their Thanksgiving meal.

"Lord, we thank you," he prayed. "We thank you for this bountiful food we have before us and ask your blessings upon it. Also, Lord, we thank you for the precious past and for the unknown future that is before us. We thank you that, because of you, we can have hope, and for those things that are in your hands that we don't understand. We pray Lord for your healing hand to touch Aimee and bring her back to us. And I thank you, Lord, for the assurance that no matter how things may appear, all will be well in the end. Amen."

"Amen," they all agreed.

Jane wiped her mouth with her napkin, "I'll bet we are the only people in the state of Indiana, or even the entire country that are having our Thanksgiving dinner in the bedroom."

They all laughed in agreement.

"I wonder if Aimee can hear us." Kendra looked over at her sister.

"I hope so," Byron said. "Let's hope that someday we'll be able to sit around the Thanksgiving table with Aimee and tell her about this extraordinary day."

Joey pointed toward the window. "It's really beginning to snow out there." He, Kendra, and Carmon left the table and ran over to the window to admire the snow.

"There is just something so special about the first snowfall each year," Carmon said.

"The flakes are so large," Kendra said.

It was a picturesque scene. The snow floated down over the back yard blanketing the trees and the pond with white.

Memories flashed through Kendra's mind as she stood there watching the falling snow. "I can remember when Aimee and I stood here in our flannel pajamas, admiring the snow."

"It doesn't seem that long ago." Byron smiled at her.

In spite of all the circumstances of the previous year, the little bedroom at Alfaland was filled with love and happiness that Thanksgiving.

Joey touched by the warmth of the moment, looked into Kendra's eyes and said, "This truly is a day of Thanksgiving."

"Yes it is," Kendra said, smiling back at him.

"Joey, I hope you're not too stuffed with all that food to sing?" Jane asked. "I've heard so much about your singing. I'm looking forward to hearing you."

"I can always sing," Joey assured her.

They gathered in the living room by the fire where Joey played his guitar and sang for them. Joey sang several songs he had written, along with several well-known gospel songs. They were all moved by the words that he sang and the beauty of his voice.

Kendra loved hearing Joey sing. He was so dear to her. She regretted that they couldn't have shared more than friendship. "There aren't many like him in this world," she thought as she listened to him sing.

They all sang several Christmas carols. Mist filled Kendra and Byron's eyes as they remembered precious past Thanksgivings with their mother and Aimee Sue. They also in times past would sing together with their mother playing the piano.

After the evening meal, while they were sitting around the kitchen table, finishing off Joey's pumpkin pie, Byron said he had an announcement to make. He stood to his feet, hesitated a moment, and glanced at Jane. She nodded at him and smiled.

"Jane and I have decided..." He stammered a bit and then continued. "...We'd like to...we'd like to get married and we're asking for your blessing," he said, looking directly at Kendra. "It just sort of happened. We both feel that Leigh would be pleased, under the circumstances, that we have each other."

Kendra was blank. The room was quiet. Although the announcement took her by surprise, Kendra had to admit that they would be good for each other. "This is going to take a little time to digest," she thought. "I'll deal with myself later. What's important now is to give Dad and Jane my blessing."

Kendra stood, walked around the table, and hugged her father. "You have my complete blessing, Dad and Jane. I do understand and love you both." She then went over and embraced Aunt Jane. "I know there's no one on this earth my mother would have wanted more for my dad. You both are very fortunate." Inside she couldn't refute the sadness that tugged at her heart. Smiling, she asked, "So when is the big day?"

"We've asked Pastor Murray to marry us here next Saturday night," Byron said smiling with admiration at Jane. "We wanted to make it as soon as possible."

"They can't mean next week," she thought. "Are they serious? Have they lost their minds?" She looked at them and forced a smile. "Sounds terrific, do I get to be here?" The way things were going she had her doubts.

"Of course, sweetheart, you better be here. We want to keep it very simple. No big deal and you are all invited." He nodded toward the others. "Dr Scott, Jeff, and his wife are going to stand up with us."

Joey couldn't keep his eyes off of Kendra. He knew her well and could read what was going through her mind. "She's going through the motions for Byron and Jane's sake," he thought to himself. "I know this has got to be a shock for her." His heart reached out to her. He loved her more than ever and made the decision, "I will not hold this inside any longer. I can't. I'm going to tell her how I feel."

That night, alone in her apartment, Kendra had a lengthy cry. She wasn't unhappy about the marriage, she was just sad for the loss of her mother. "Again, more changes," she thought, "I wish I could talk to Joey." Loneliness crept over her. She spotted the little teddy bear lying on the bookcase headboard. It made her smile. The alarm on the watch had gone off two days before. Her thoughts turned to Jared. "I wish that Jared was here." She felt confused. She hated it when she felt like this.

Her mind turned yet again to Joey.

At ten-thirty, she found herself dialing Joey's house. To her surprise, a girl answered and Kendra hung up without saying anything. "I should leave him alone," she thought. "He's got a life and I need to go on with my life. From now on I'll leave him alone."

Joey walked out of the bathroom. "I told you I was going to the Patton's for Thanksgiving."

"After today," Julie said, "We're finished. I can't believe how you just drop everything to go to that spoiled brat Kendra's for Thanksgiving. I really thought you'd show up at my parents. You won't have to worry about me anymore, Joey, I'm out of here."

"I'm going out for awhile," Joey said.

"I won't be here when you get back," Julie said. She stared at him. "You don't even care, do you?"

Joey said nothing and walked out the door. His heart was on fire after being with Kendra all day. He decided he couldn't wait any longer. He was going to tell Kendra how he felt tonight. He pulled his Corvette up in front of her apartment, turned off the lights and sat there. Her lights were out. "I'm being crazy," he said to himself. "What am I doing?"

He pulled out of the parking lot and drove back to his house. When he arrived home, Julie was gone.

Chapter Eleven

"Guess what?" Jared's voice radiated over the phone. "I am almost there; I just got into Indianapolis about an hour ago! If it weren't for the fact that I have to load up the U-Haul in the morning I'd leave right now. I'm so anxious to see you!"

"You don't know how good it is to hear your voice," Kendra said. "Teddy hasn't been doing his job so good lately."

"I'll have to have a talk with that little bear. Of course, after today you won't need him anymore. You'll have the real Jared. That is if you still want me."

"Yes," Kendra said, "I sure do."

"So how was Thanksgiving at Alfaland with your family? I hope yours was better than mine." He sighed. "I don't think I've ever had such a lousy Thanksgiving. My dinner consisted of a meat loaf platter at a little diner somewhere between San Jose and Oakland."

"I was hoping you'd call." Kendra sat down on the bed and leaned up against the headboard.

"I did, Kendra, but it was earlier in the evening. I figured you must have still been out at your father's. Then, by the time I got a room, it was getting pretty late, so I hated to bother you. I figured you'd be tired from your busy day."

Kendra told him about her father's announcement and the wedding planned for the following day. "I was shocked. I knew they were close, but, not that close. Do you think you could be back in time to go with me? I'd really like for you to be there. It would mean a lot to me if you could."

"I'll make it a point to be there if you really want me. I'd be honored. So you were surprised, huh? How do you feel about this? Your dad's getting married, I mean."

"I've had mixed feelings about it," she admitted. "At first, I was very surprised and then a little depressed, mainly because it makes it so final that Mother and Dad will never be again. But I am happy for them. They seem like they are really happy and excited. You know what; I'm feeling so much better just knowing that you'll be here soon."

"What time are they getting married?" Jared asked.

"They are getting married at five so they can catch their plane." She reached over and patted Buster's head. He had walked in and sat down beside the bed. "Maybe, if you could, be here by three."

"I can make it, no problem. I'll have to get ready at your place, is that okay? I'm homeless right at the moment, or, I can go to mother's."

"No, you come here. I don't want to wait that long."

"Okay, I'll see you tomorrow about 3:00."

They hung up and Kendra got busy tidying up the apartment.

Jared appeared in front of her apartment about two-thirty Saturday afternoon. She ran outside in her bare feet to greet him. When he stepped out of his jeep, she threw her arms around his neck. Jared, pleased and touched by her excitement, picked her up off the ground and whirled her around as they embraced. He carried her in his arms into the apartment and, once he had kicked the door shut behind them, kissed her. Emotions that they had both felt before his departure flooded back, now that they were together again.

"I'm a man without a home at the moment. All I have in this world is out there in that little U-Haul and my Jeep." Jared shook his head in disbelief. "Sure makes a person realize how little they have. Well, I think I better get ready," he said. He ran outside to his Jeep, picked out some clothes to wear and then went into the bathroom to take a shower.

Hearing him humming and whistling as he showered brought a smile to her face. "It is good to have him back," she thought.

Kendra went in her bedroom and finished putting the final touches on her make up She dressed fairly casual since her father had said he wanted to keep it simple.

She heard the shower door slide open and a few moments later Jared walked out of the bathroom with a towel wrapped around his waist; his long blond hair in wet disarray. Kendra yielded to an uncontrollable desire to stare at him. Jared sensed her eyes surveying his body. He stopped, stared into her eyes for a moment, then walked across the room and wrapped his long muscular arms around her to pull her against his bare chest. Jared held her like a precious treasure. His wet curly hair smelled of the fresh aroma of shampoo and dripped a drop of water on her cheek and nose.

"I've missed you so," he said. "For some reason I had this terrible fear that I wouldn't see you again. I'm so thankful to finally be here."

She slid her fingers across his shoulders and secured them behind his damp neck. "I'm so thankful you're here, too."

Kendra left and he finished getting ready. When he emerged from the bedroom he looked extremely handsome. He was wearing a dark green sports jacket with a light green shirt. "You look great," Kendra informed him.

"You look beautiful yourself," he replied. "I'm ready if you are."

They arrived at Alfaland at four o'clock. Mr. Patton displayed no reaction to Jared's being with Kendra but he was a little surprised. He had thought Jared had left the picture because he hadn't heard Kendra mention him.

"I'm so very proud of you, Father." She smiled and gave him a hug. "You look very handsome." Byron was wearing a dark brown suit. His skin was tanned. His thick dark hair was only showing slight signs of graying around the temples.

The wedding took place in the living room in front of the fireplace. Byron winked and smiled at Kendra as he stood waiting for Jane. The room was decorated with bouquets of fall colors and candles. Jane, wearing a soft yellow floor length cotton gown entered from the stars. The joy on her face was stunning. Kendra had never seen her more beautiful.

The ceremony was simple, but moving. The words that her father and Jane shared from the heart convinced Kendra that this was a good road her father had chosen. She knew he would be happy. That was all she desired for him.

After a brief reception on the front porch, the small group of family and friends sent the newlyweds off. Dr. Scott and his wife took them to the airport in Fort Wayne to catch their plane for Hawaii where they would be honeymooning for a couple of weeks. In spite of the fact that it was a joyous event, Kendra couldn't help but feel emotional when her father and Jane drove off. Jared, sensing her thoughts, wrapped his arm around her shoulder and held her as they stood watching the car drive down the long drive and disappear into the night. Her family was never going to be the same again. Another page had turned.

All Joey wanted to do was get out of there. It took every ounce of strength that he had just to speak and be cordial. "What is going on?" he thought. "Somewhere between yesterday and today my dreams have been shattered; I can see that this is more than a casual acquaintance between Kendra and Jared. How could this have happened right under my nose?" The worst pain was that he had brought this man into their lives. Joey's eyes were filled with tears as he drove away from Alfaland. His heart filled with a pain and loss that he knew he would never get over. "My days in Fort Akers are numbered," he said to himself, "I couldn't stand the pain of being near her day after day and continuing this pretense."

"Before we leave," Kendra said to Jared, "I want to run upstairs and see Aimee."

"I'll go with you," he said.

Kendra stood beside the bed holding Aimee's lifeless hand in hers. Jared watched as Kendra laid her hand on Aimee's slightly protruding abdomen.

"I can feel tiny little kicks tapping against my hand. Feel this." She smiled, grabbed his hand, and then laid it on Aimee's abdomen.

"No, don't. Its' not right," he said. He felt the tiny little taps under his hand before pulling away. "I'm sorry; I just don't feel its right for me to touch her when she doesn't know it. This whole thing is so sad."

Kendra laid her head on the side of his shoulder. "It's okay, Jared. I know Aimee wouldn't mind." She could smell the luscious aroma of his cologne. She was moved by his sensitivity.

Jared smiled at Kendra with a tender compassion then slid his hand up under her hair to massage the back of her neck. "It is such a feeling of helplessness. I have a surprise for you. Maybe it will cheer you up a little."

"What is it?" she asked.

"I'll show you when we get back to your apartment."

They stopped and picked up a pizza before returning to Kendra's apartment.

"You carry the pizza," Jared said, "I'll get the surprise." He waited until she was inside, then lifted a rectangular object out of the back of the Jeep and carried it inside behind her.

She laid the pizza on the table. "What is it?"

"You sit over there." He pointed to a chair and lifted the large package up onto the sofa. "And, close your eyes."

Kendra sat down on the chair, crossed her legs, folded her arms across her lap and then closed her eyes. She could hear him humming to himself as he ripped the paper.

After a few seconds, he said, "Okay, you can open them."

Kendra's mouth dropped. She jumped up. "I don't believe it," she said. "It's the painting of the horse in the moonlight that your mother painted. It's so beautiful." She hesitated for a moment. "Your mother didn't mind?" She walked over to the couch where he was holding the painting.

"I can talk my mother into anything." He grinned. "But she also thought this was an excellent idea."

"Thank you," she said, tilting her head and placing her hand on his shoulder. "This means so much to me. I'm going to hang it right there, above the sofa."

"I'll hang it for you;" he smiled and patted his pocket. "I even brought the hooks."

"That is nice. My mother is so good," Jared said after he'd completed the task and backed up to look at it. The couple stood in the center of the room, her arm around his waist, his around her shoulder, admiring the painting.

"Our pizza's getting cold," Kendra reminded him. She grabbed his hand and led him into the kitchen.

"How about doing some Christmas shopping with me tomorrow?" Jared asked. We could leave early and spend the entire day. Maybe we could go to Fort Wayne, if that sounds okay?"

"That's a great idea. I haven't even thought about Christmas. It's time I do." She took a bite of a potato chip. "You know this is the big shopping weekend of the year. It could be crowded, but I kind of like the crowds and the excitement."

"At Christmas time, I have to admit, I do too!" Jared said.

Returning to the living room, they sat together on the leather chair to enjoy the painting. Kendra ran her hand over the back of his head, stroking his long blond hair. She placed her hands on both sides of his head and kissed him on the cheek.

"Thank you for the painting. I do love it." Kendra felt relaxed and natural being with him.

After Jared had left for his mothers in South Bend, Kendra went to bed filled with a contentment that she hadn't felt for many months.

The atmosphere at the mall was exhilarating and hectic. There were busy shoppers with their bags and packages hurrying in and out of stores. Kendra loved this time of year and the joy of being with Jared made it all the more special. They stopped to browse at a JC Penney store and bought a Notre Dame sweatshirt for Kendra's father and Jared's boss, and spent several minutes at the jewelry store where Jared purchased a ring for his mother and Kendra purchased a tennis bracelet for Carmon and Jane. They wondered into a toy store just to look at the toys. Kendra enjoyed looking at the dolls and Jared liked the toy trains. "I've always wanted to set up a model train track." Jared said. "Someday I just might do that, if I ever have the space," then added, "and time."

Exhausted, they bought some tacos and sat down by the ice rink to eat, and rest. "I'm beat!" Kendra confessed. She put her purse and bags on the empty chair.

The Christmas carol echoed over the loudspeakers in the mall. "O holy night, the stars are brightly shining. It is the night of our dear savior's birth. Long live the world in peace and..."

They listened to the music and watched a number of skaters swerving back and forth across the ice rink.

"We have accomplished a lot." Kendra wiped her mouth with her napkin after completing the last bite of her taco. She smiled. "I like shopping with you. You're fun."

He picked up the papers on the table and put them in the sack then took the last sip of his drink. "You look like a Christmas Bunny," he said.

"A Christmas Bunny?" She laughed. "Is that good?" Kendra was wearing a white fur jacket and hat. Her long dark hair dangled loosely over her shoulders.

Jared smiled in admiration at her across the little table. "You look absolutely adorable." He leaned over the table and gave her a kiss.

She smiled back at him, "You look pretty terrific yourself, Mr. Bradley." She eyed his black leather coat, tan sweater and jeans, with black boots. Kendra believed he was the most handsome man she had ever seen.

It was heavily snowing by the time they got back to her apartment. They unloaded all their packages, let Buster out, and then headed out to Alfaland to check in with Sarah and Judy. Kendra had promised her father she would keep an eye on things while they were gone. The snow was getting so heavy that Jared had to turn on the wipers to clear the window.

"That's strange," Kendra said as they drove up the long drive toward the house. "There aren't any lights on."

"Could they have gone to bed this early?" Jared asked.

Kendra felt uneasy. "I wouldn't have thought so."

Jared drove on around the circle drive and stopped with the lights of the Jeep shinning toward the back porch. There were several footprints in the snow.

"There are tire tracks in the drive also," Jared said. He left the lights on and they walked up to the back door.

Kendra tried the door, but it was locked so she dug through her purse and pulled out a key. She unlocked the door. It was cold inside. No one had turned up the heat. She reached for the light switch and turned on the kitchen light. They noticed a paper on the table. It was a note from Sarah.

Kendra, we tried to reach you. We had the ambulance take Aimee to the hospital. Dr. Scott thinks that they will have to take the baby soon. Please come to the hospital right away...Sarah

Chapter Twelve

Kendra and Jared entered the waiting room at the hospital. Judy jumped up and rushed over when she spotted them.

"She's in surgery!" she said. "I'm so glad you got here. Aimee's water broke about three o'clock, just out of the blue."

Sarah joined them, "And then she started bleeding. We called the ambulance and Dr. Scott right away. We tried to call you."

"I am sorry," Kendra said. She took hold of both of the ladies' hands, "I should have thought to let you know I would be out of town. Or, I could have taken my cell phone. I didn't even think about her having the baby this soon."

"We were surprised, too." Judy said.

The waiting room was empty except for the four of them. Jared managed to find them a pot of coffee and some plastic cups.

Dr. Scott appeared in the waiting room at seven forty-five. His eyes lit up when he saw Kendra.

"Kendra, I'm so glad you're here." He sat down on the chair next to her and placed his hefty hands around hers. "You have a new little boy in your family. He is perfectly fine, just a little small. He's only four and a half pounds, but everything appears normal. Aimee's doing okay, no more problems, other then what we were anticipating. Of course, it will take a while to heal, but hopefully everything will heal up just fine."

Kendra stared straight ahead for several seconds digesting the reality of it all. She was in awe. She then turned to the doctor. "Can we see him?"

"You sure can," Dr. Scott led them down the hall to the nursery.

Kendra felt a little nervous. Jared took hold of her hand as they walked. When the reached the nursery he squeezed her hand to let her know he was there for her. She had a tense smile as they entered the room.

"He's in the incubator." Dr. Scott pointed to the incubator in the corner of the room, where there were three other babies in beds. "For now, but he shouldn't have to be there long."

Kendra gasped. "What a precious little doll." She whispered as to not awaken the other babies in the room. Mist filled her eyes. "He's so little and look at all that hair. He's beautiful."

"He is beautiful," Jared said, staring at the little figure sleeping in the incubator. He was fighting back tears in his own eyes.

"Has anyone thought of a name?" Dr. Scott asked in a whisper.

"Yes," Kendra said, Ian. That's the name she had wanted me to name my baby if it was a boy. I know she'd like that. This has all happened sooner than we had anticipated. We are going to have to get some things around and make some plans." She looked toward the doctor. "How long will they be here?"

"I'd say a week or two for the baby and maybe two weeks for Aimee," Dr. Scott said. "This is going to be quite a surprise for your dad and Jane."

"What about Aimee? Jared asked Dr. Scott. "How long do you think she'll be in this coma?"

"I just cannot predict, Jared," he said, shaking his head. "She could go on like this a year, two years, or she could wake up tomorrow. I honestly have no answer."

Sarah and Judy left the hospital at ten. They agreed to stay around Alfaland and take care of things. Kendra told them before they left that she would keep them posted.

"We'll be there whenever you need, and we'll keep things in order till your father gets home," Judy said.

"We have no where to go," Sarah added.

Kendra and Jared lingered at the hospital for some time after Sarah and Judy had left and went in and sat with Aimee before leaving. Kendra sat down on a wooden chair by Aimee's bed. Before speaking, she laid her head on Aimee's arm and cried. After gaining her composure, she held Aimee's hand and told her about her precious little son.

"Sis, you may be able to hear me. I don't know. If you do I want to tell you that you have a beautiful baby boy. Aimee he's so tiny and has lots of beautiful hair. Dr. Scott says he's doing just fine and so are you." Kendra felt a lump come up in her throat. "Aimee, don't worry. We'll take care of little Ian for you. He won't be alone. We'll love him for you." Kendra couldn't speak anymore. She quietly sat for several minutes, holding Aimee's hand.

Jared stood behind her with his hands on her shoulders. Seeing the pain that she was going through was more than he could stand. Kendra was unaware of the warm tears that streamed down his own cheeks as he stood behind her.

They were both quiet for sometime when they arrived back at Kendra's apartment. The situation was a lot to absorb.

"That is one lovely boy." Jared said, "I just wanted to pick him up and love him. He seems so helpless and alone laying there."

"I know what you mean. It's just so sad. He has no father or mother."

They went to the kitchen to prepare themselves a couple of ham sandwiches.

Jared grew quiet and deep in thought while he stood at the kitchen counter, slicing a hunk of Colby cheese. He stopped and laid down the knife. He stared at the refrigerator for a moment and then turned toward Kendra.

"You know I've fallen in love with you, don't you? It's crazy as hell, but I have no doubt that I love you and want to spend the rest of my life with you. I know that's not taking it slow like I had promised, but, I feel like I'm going to burst if I don't tell you that I love you." He walked over to where she was standing by the table. He kissed her, first on the forehead, then moving to her cheeks and nose and chin. He held her face in his hand and kissed her lips.

"Oh Jared, I know it's crazy, but I do feel the same," Kendra said. "But, it scares me, the way I feel. I'm so happy and confused. We've only known each other such a short time."

"Maybe it's just that we've found each other and we both know it," Jared said. "Time has nothing to do with it. When it happens, it happens."

"Please don't ever leave me. I'm scared that I'll lose you, too." Her head fell against his chest.

Jared laid his hand over the side of her face as it rested on his chest. "I will never leave you! I'm here, I'm alive, and I love you very much. Sweetheart, we both know that we have no choice over death but, as long as I'm living, I can promise I will never leave you. I do understand how you feel. I know it's hard after what you've been through, but you've got to go on and live again. Look at your dad." Jared kissed her again. "Please don't deny us a future because of the past. This entire situation is strange. Why don't we just grab it and make something good out of it? Let's take that little one in and raise him. He needs us, and I'd love him as if he were my own. Like the doctor said, Aimee could be in this condition for years. We're the best answer for a home for little Ian."

Kendra walked over to where he was sitting. She held him to her breast. She kissed the top of his head. "Where did you come from, Mr. Bradley? Having you walk into my life is the best thing that could possibly have happened." She stared down into his blue eyes. "Are you sure about the baby?" she asked. "This year has taught me that life is short and precious, and I don't want to waste a second of it. I do love you, Jared. I don't want to wait. Let's get married right away."

"Sweetheart, I agree, I'll do the best I can to be a good husband to you. There is something that you need to know that I haven't mentioned." He became serious. "I have been married before." He searched her eyes for a response. "That is why I was so down before I met you. I was married for two years to my childhood sweetheart. Her name is Jessica. We had gone together all through high school and I never thought anything would come between us, but she left me last January for another man. It's been very hard for me to get over it, but meeting you has changed all that. I just wanted you to know. I didn't intend to keep it from you. There was just never a good time to bring it up."

Kendra slipped into the chair across from him. "I don't have a problem with that," she assured him. "Do you know where she is or do you ever see her?"

"No she's moved to California," he said, "with her new love. She left and never looked back." Jared looked down at the tabletop and took his fingernail to scrape off a small fleck on the table. He looked back up into her eyes. "I was devastated."

"Have you had any relationships since?" Kendra asked.

"Yes one, but oddly." He looked down at the table again, then back up at Kendra. "She left me also. I thought we had something going for us but, it didn't turn out that way. I was beginning to think I'm a loser."

"I don't know how anyone could ever leave you, Jared."

He reached across the table and took her hand.

Kendra picked up his hand, holding it as if it were some rare treasure, and then kissed the top of his fingers. She shook her head. "Where do we begin? We have to get baby things and make wedding plans. Besides that, you've got your new business to begin." Kendra threw up her hands, and then smiled at him from across the table. "I guess the first thing is for me to phone Carmon and Joey tomorrow and take some time off of work. We'll need to do some serious shopping. We'll need all the baby things and I want to get a special dress for our wedding." She grinned at him, "I'm babbling aren't I?"

Jared motioned for her to set on his lap. She did.

"You're just happy and excited. That is definitely better than being lonely and bored." Their lips met. "Why don't we begin a list of what we have to do and then, just do it? I'll make us a pot of coffee." He patted her on the rear and jumped up. "And you get us a paper and pencil. Let's get started! Number one, but not this week, we'll need to find a place to live."

Kendra agreed. "But for now we'll just stay here. We'll be okay. We'll want the baby in our room, for a while anyway, and I do have the extra bedroom. I guess we'll have to put your things in there. That are in the U-Haul, I mean."

"What about Buster?" Jared asked. At the sound of his name, Buster's ears perked up and his tail wagged for a moment before he yawned and laid his head back down.

"He'll be all right, I'm sure, but like you said, we'll need to get a bigger place soon. If need be, he could stay out at Alfaland for a while. He is happy out there. Another thing I was thinking about," she said, "I'd like to fire you from the job that I hired you for. At this point I'm ready to halt the search for the mystery man. If he'd wanted to he could have found her by now. To be honest, now that we've made the decision to take the baby, I hope he never shows up. Course, could he do anything if he did?"

"Consider me fired. I don't think he could do anything. I'm really not sure. We could check if you'd like, but I don't think there's anything to worry about."

The new lovers sat at the kitchen table with their feet propped up on each other's chairs, drinking coffee and discussing their future plans late into the night. They were exhausted, but happy.

"What are you thinking about?" Jared took a hold of her foot and began to massage it.

She turned her head and looked into his eyes. "I was just wondering where our lives were going to lead. What is going to happen in the future? Before last year I was so secure. Nothing bad had ever happened in my life. Now I know how unpredictable life is and how vulnerable we are. It's sort of scary. Do you know what I mean?"

"Yes, I do sweetheart. You've been wounded and it's going to take some time to heal. I'm going to be here to help you with that. I've never been one to worry much about tomorrow. I live for today. I don't know if that's good or bad but it's the way I am. I'll tell you what sweetheart, I believe we can overcome any obstacle that comes into our lives, and together we can face any situation that may be dealt us in the future."

She stroked his face with her hand. "I love you so, Jared. "I'm going to do everything in my power to make you as happy."

Chapter Thirteen

The months that followed were full and happy ones for the new Bradley family. The marriage took place the week before Christmas at the Patton farm; with little baby Ian in a basket on the couch. He was a healthy, alert and good-natured little boy. As a wedding present Byron had arranged a honeymoon in Hawaii for Kendra and Jared along with the offer that he and Jane would keep baby Ian while they were gone. In January, they moved into a larger three-bedroom apartment that became available in the same complex. Jared's dream of becoming a police officer became a reality in March when he was hired to work for the Fort Akers Police Department. A small town department was exactly what he had always hoped for. He also enjoyed the fact that he was near to home. The only disadvantages to the position were, as a rookie, he was forced to rotate shifts, and he was required to cut his beautiful hair short.

"Thankfully, Sampson, you sure didn't lose any of your strength because of the hair cut" Kendra nuzzled up next to him in bed. "If anything, you may be gaining some."

"I aim to please, sweetheart. It's my burdensome duty," he said.

"I saw Carmon today," she said.

"So, how is she doing without you?"

Kendra had made the decision not to go back to the beauty shop after her marriage because of her added responsibilities as a parent and becoming more involved at the *Gazette*. They were expanding their coverage to two more counties, and Joey's interest in the paper appeared to be dwindling.

"She's found a new direction in her life, also. Do you recall that German shepherd that she purchased for herself at Christmas?"

Jared nodded.

"She's enrolled the dog in obedience school and has managed to become romantically involved with the instructor, Charlie Williams." Kendra laughed. "He's a divorcee with two kids and he's ten years her senior." She turned her head and looked at Jared. "Can you believe it? Carmon with two boys?"

"Life is full of surprises. That's great." He turned on his side and stoked her forehead, pushing a group of hairs off her cheek. "From what you've told me, Carmon was lonely and she needed someone in her life. I know she's been a pretty special friend to you." He caressed her hair with his fingertips.

A long contented sigh came from the little crib that was across the room from them. Kendra and Jared both turned to check. Seeing Ian was sound asleep, they looked at each other and grinned.

"He must be dreaming." Jared rolled over on his back.

Kendra turned over on her side putting her arm on his chest and one leg between his legs. Her expression turned serious. "It appears our honeymoon was a productive one, along with being extremely enjoyable." She hesitated, and then ran her finger down his chest. "You, Mr. Bradley, are about to become a father."

Jared's eyes lit up. He grabbed her shoulders. "For sure, we're going to have a baby?"

Kendra grinned and nodded.

"Oh, honey, that's great. I can't believe all the things in my life that have happened since I've met you. I've got it all." He pulled her up to meet his lips. "What about your condition, I mean after losing the last baby the way you did? Could there be any problems?"

"Dr. Scott doesn't foresee any. He just suggests that I have regular check-ups, just to make sure."

"That settles it. I think it's time we get serious about looking for a house."

She smiled and kissed his nose. "I think you're right, sweetheart. Oh, I almost forgot, Dad called today. They want to talk to us about something. I told him we'd stop out tomorrow night so he invited us to dinner."

"Did he say what about?"

"No, he didn't seem to want to talk about it over the phone. I'm a little curious. You never know with those two. It is good to see them so happy, though."

The couple's lips united once more before they floated off to sleep, Kendra's head still resting on his chest.

The aroma of spring filled the evening breeze at Alfaland. It was the first week in May and the lengthy drive way was lined with blooming multicolored tulips, which seemed to sing with color. They were complemented by the fragrance of hyacinths and lilac bushes, which were in full bloom.

"It's hard for me to decide which season I love the most out here," Kendra said. She turned to check if Ian was awake in his car seat. He was, chewing on a blue baby rattle that he held in his hand.

"So, do you have any idea why your dad and Jane want to see us?" Jared asked. He pulled to a stop behind an old John Deer tractor that was parked in the drive.

"Not a clue. I just hope nothing is wrong. Like I said, Daddy just phoned and said he wanted to discuss something with us and invited us to dinner."

"Since it's such a beautiful evening I've set up the table on the front porch," Jane said when they walked in the back door. She took Ian from Kendra and kissed him. "We're getting to be terribly fond of this little guy." They had been keeping Ian most of the days when Kendra worked.

After dinner, Kendra placed Ian in his nearby baby swing and the adults retired to the porch's white wicker furniture.

"I suppose you've been wondering what this is all about." Byron sat down beside his wife. "Let me explain. Jane and I have been doing a lot of talking, and thinking, the last few months about what we'd like to do with the years we have left. We've come to a couple of conclusions, and some of them involve you two. We'd really like to start doing some traveling, some in the U.S., and maybe some overseas." He reached over and placed his hand on Jane's knee. "We've even thought about buying one of those motor homes and traveling the states. Who knows? We are both ready and we feel that we are not getting any younger." He smiled at Jane. "What we wanted to talk to you about is to offer you a proposition. We both agree that we don't want a lot of responsibility or property to keep up with anymore, but we also don't want to sell Alfaland to some strangers and there's the situation with Aimee." His head dropped for a moment, then he looked up at Jane and then over toward Kendra and Jared. "We were wondering and hoping that you two might consider moving out here and taking over the property and caring for Aimee. What with your new little one coming along, you are going to need more room. We realize the lack of privacy would be a sacrifice, but honestly it's not bad. Sarah and Judy spend most of their evenings in their room. As a matter of fact, we've already discussed this with them and they are willing to take over a larger role here if you would like, such as cooking and laundry, etcetera. They agree they are not that busy with Aimee and are willing to take over more household duties. I've informed them, and I want it to be clear to you both, that I will be taking care of their salaries if you are willing to make the move."

"Don't forget about George," Jane said.

"Oh yeah, George has also agreed to stay on and take care of the horses and any maintenance around the farm."

"And," Jane said, "Lydia Ann is willing to baby sit for Ian, when we are not around." She had quit school when she was sixteen, as was their custom.

Byron continued. "We understand how busy you both are with your occupations and that this would create quite a load for you so we've tried to cover all the bases to make it as easy as possible."

Kendra was stunned. She looked at Jared for a response.

He hesitated for a moment then said, "I can't think of any place on earth I'd rather live." Jared looked back at Kendra. "How do you feel, honey? What do you think?"

"Sounds like a good deal to me. It appears you have taken care of all the loose ends, Dad. How can we say no? I love Alfaland."

"I can't believe this. I just can't believe it." Jared said as they made the drive back to Fort Akers. "Alfaland, it's the most beautiful place I've ever seen. I can't believe that I'm actually going to live there."

"My mind is spinning." Kendra said. "This is such a shock. Somehow I've always had the feeling that someday I'd end up at Alfaland but that was somewhere way off in the future."

"Do you think we can handle it? Aimee and all, I mean? And, not being alone?"

She looked at him with some question in her eyes. "That's the only bad part."

"I do have to wonder how the situation with Aimee is going to end up, don't you?"

He pulled the Jeep up and parked in front of their apartment. "Yeah, she just seems to stay the same."

Kendra exited the vehicle and lifted Ian, who was sound asleep, from his car seat. "It's so sad. Aimee's lost such a big chunk out of her life already. I wonder how long this will go on." She draped the diaper bag over her other shoulder and began walking toward the apartment. "To be honest, I've almost given up hope, but you know someday she might just wake up. I can't imagine what that would be like for her, and for us."

Jared grabbed the diaper bag, closed the Jeep door behind her and then walked ahead to unlock the apartment door. "I have to admit I'm a little uncomfortable about not being alone, but I think we can work it out," Jared said.

"Did you hear Jane telling me before we left that they already have a two bedroom condo picked out in Fort Akers near the golf course." She took Ian in the bedroom and placed him in his crib.

Jared followed her. "They aren't going to waste anytime, are they? I guess they feel they have a lot of living to do." He leaned over and kissed Ian on the forehead. "I admire them for that. I guess we'll just go for it and see what happens." Kendra undressed, slipped into one of Jared's t-shirts and then crawled into bed.

"I wish I didn't have to go to work." Jared caressed her soft cheek with the top of his fingers and kissed her goodnight. He went into the bathroom to get ready.

"I do too." She rolled over on her side, attempting to go to sleep, but her mind churned over the events that had developed in the last few hours.

The momentous move to Alfaland took place the following month. It was an exciting experience, even though somewhat of an adjustment for everyone concerned.

"It's so strange to have all this space." Jared said. He smiled at her and headed back out through the kitchen to get another box. "This place was definitely built for a large family," The house had six bedrooms, three baths, a huge three-car garage, and a recreation room in the basement, which had rarely been used the last several years.

"We're going to have to work hard to fill it up." Jared spoke in a seductive manner then grabbed her around the waist to push against her while she reached into the trunk to get another box.

"Sweetheart," she said, "you are going to have to watch it."

"There's nobody around, and you look so sexy in those shorts."

"George could be in the barn," she said grinning.

He kissed the back of her shoulder. "I am going to have to adjust to this." He moved his hands from around her waist and grabbed another box to carry inside. "Maybe I should put my shirt back on, Sarah and Judy might see something." He had taken it off earlier and thrown it over a kitchen chair.

Kendra slapped his side. "Stop it. You're all right." Kendra took a moment to admire his broad shoulders and firm biceps. It was evident that he had been working out at the department almost daily. She ran her finger down his chest. "This is going to be an adjustment." They stole another moment to kiss before continuing.

The decision was made that they would take the larger bedroom on the main floor, the one that had been her father's, and give little Ian the smaller bedroom located next to theirs.

Sunday was their first complete day at Alfaland. Kendra and Jared had slipped out of bed early because there was so much work they needed to get done before going back to work the following day.

"He's still sound asleep," Kendra said walking into the kitchen after checking on Ian. She poured them both a second cup of coffee. "Apparently being in the new surroundings didn't affect him any."

"He was out cold when I carried him to bed last night, but it was pretty late. Come here." Jared motioned for her to set on his lap.

Kendra ignored his request and seated herself across the table from him.

He looked up from his coffee cup, "Where's the Sunday paper? Do we get a paper out here?"

"It's out in the mail box, my dear. Someone has to go get it." She brushed back a long string of hair that fell from her pony tail and across her face.

"All the way out there?" he asked. "It hadn't occurred to me that country people have some inconveniences. We'll have to go all the way to the road to get our mail, too? Won't we? You know that never entered my mind. What would happen if we just put our mail box up here by the house?"

"Then, love, we'd never get any mail." She couldn't help but chuckle at his concern.

"I have an idea. Maybe we could train Buster to do this job," he said, rubbing Buster's head. Jared put his shoes on and left with the dog to walk, what he claimed, was a mile to get the Sunday paper.

"Well," he said when he came back inside. "If that's the biggest inconvenience, it's minor. Beside, the walk was beautiful and the exercise is good for me."

More and more as the months flew by they, including Ian, grew to love living at Alfaland. Ian was curious and fascinated with absolutely everything: birds, horses, water, trees, grass, and especially dirt. He loved playing and digging in dirt. From the beginning, they agreed to make every effort to keep the fact clear in Ian's mind that Aimee Sue was his natural mother. They wanted him to understand so that he would not be shocked by anything that could happen in the future. He had been given the name Ian Patton from birth.

Aimee Leigh Bradley was born on October eighteenth at three in the morning. She was a healthy, blond, curly haired, nine and one half pound girl. Jared entered the waiting room where his mother and Carmon had been waiting for the last hour and a half.

He embraced his mother, "We have a little girl!" He shook his head in disbelief, "Oh, mom, she is a doll." His blue eyes glistened with pride.

At hearing the news, Lori, half laughing and half crying, embraced her son. "My first grandchild. Son, I'm so proud and happy. I finally located Byron and Jane in Colorado Springs and told them we'd let them know as soon as we had the news. Why don't you go give them a call?" She handed him a small piece of paper she had in her jacket pocket. "Can we go in and see Kendra?"

"You bet. I just came from there. She'd be pleased to see you."

Carmon and Lori made their way down the hall and into Kendra's room. Her eyes lit when they entered. "Have you seen her yet?" Kendra asked. "She's a beauty." Her heart swelled with pride.

"Not yet, we wanted to check in on you first," Carmon said. She hugged her friend. "You look pretty chipper for just having a baby."

Kendra turned her head on her pillow and smiled at her friend of many years. "It must be because I'm so happy." Even so, signs of exhaustion were evident in her voice and eyes.

Lori's love for her daughter-in-law was apparent. She wrapped her arms around Kendra. "You have been so good for my son. I've never seen Jared as complete and happy as he's been since you came into his life." Lori's eyes were again filled with tears of joy. She handed Kendra a little bag of assorted personal goodies that she had prepared.

Kendra noticed how vibrant and beautiful Lori was. "I love your son very much," she said to Lori.

"I know you do. Why don't you rest now?" She stroked Kendra's forehead. Her hair was still damp and in disarray. "We'll be back tomorrow." The two women left to go see baby Aimee Leigh.

Sarah and Judy attended to their needs when they returned home from the hospital. Kendra hugged each one of them when she walked back into the kitchen after tucking Ian in for the second time. "You two are definitely a godsend, especially since Aimee Leigh's been born. You are so good to me, and to us."

"Your father is paying us quite handsomely to do this," Judy admitted. "Sometimes we feel guilty for taking his money because we're enjoying it too much."

"We feel we should be doing more." Sarah said while attempting to slide a food processor up onto a shelf that was just a little beyond her reach. Kendra grabbed it and finished placing it in the cabinet for her. Sarah and Judy were both on the short and stocky side.

"I feel like you're family," Kendra said.

"The feeling is mutual," Judy assured her.

Kendra walked back into the living room where Jared sat in her father's old recliner with Aimee Leigh on his chest, the same as he had been doing with Ian over the past several months. He was almost asleep himself with his large hand resting on his daughter's back.

He looked over at Kendra and smiled. "I like being a father. It sure meant a lot to me today when so many of the guys stopped, including Chief Troyer. I was proud." He stroked the back of Aimee's small head, placed his finger under her tiny hand and then wiggled it, causing no effect or reaction from the contented little body on his chest.

"I'm a little disappointed that Joey hasn't come to see her. Did you see the large picture of her and I that he ran in the paper? He must have gotten it from the hospital."

"I'm the guilty one there. I gave him the picture. He did stop by the hospital to see the baby."

"I'll get you back for that," she teased. "It did make me feel good though, but a little embarrassed. He didn't have to make it such a large photo."

"Kendra, are you aware of the fact that man was in love with you when we met?"

"What are you talking about?"

"I really wasn't sure if you realized it or not. I could see it that night at your father's wedding. I'm just thankful that I ended up with you."

Kendra stared at him, still a little stunned. She wasn't sure how to respond. "I'm not convinced you're right about that, Jared."

"It's just an observation. It's in the past." He changed the subject. "Why don't you come and get this little bundle of joy so I can get up. Let's go to bed."

Chapter Fourteen

"Stand by after this announcement for the newest country music favorite that is leaping in the country music charts all over the U.S.A." The local radio station disk jockey announced.

Jared was back to work, and Kendra had just finished feeding Aimee Leigh. She then put Ian and Aimee Leigh down for a nap. She had turned the radio to her favorite local station and proceeded to do some much need cleaning in their bedroom. It was the only area that Sarah and Judy didn't touch.

"Here it is folks." The D.J. came back on the air. "We've been getting requests for this one all day. Fort Akers' own, Joey Dubious, with his hot new and growing hit, 'When Love Dies'. Ladies and gentlemen, here it is. We are proud of you Joey."

Kendra nearly lost her balance. She grabbed the corner of her poster bed and sat down to listen. Unintended tears streamed down her cheeks. A chill rippled down her spine as she listened to Joey's beautiful words and voice flowing from the speaker on the radio.

Where love has gone, who can know?
Why love dies instead of grows.
Where love has gone, no one knows
Why love dies instead of grows.
I reach out in my dreams and remember
What once was alive to me.
A love, a hope, a future;
A life that will now never be.
Where love has gone, who can know?
Why love dies instead of grows.
Where love has gone, no one knows
Why love dies instead of grows.

Kendra was glued to the bed where she sat, listening to the entire song. When the music was over, Kendra felt a sadness come over her that she didn't understand. Maybe it was because, at that moment, she came to the realization in her heart that Joey would be leaving Fort Akers, the newspaper and her. "It's understandable," she thought, "with a song and voice so beautiful, Joey's life is going to change dramatically. Why hadn't he said anything?" He had been so much a part of her life ever since she could remember and even more so after Aaron died.

She walked over and stood for several minutes staring out the back bedroom window overlooking the pond, fields and woods. The leaves had reached their peak the previous week, but the colors were still striking. Kendra folded her arms and placed them on the top of the center frame of the window. She rested her chin on her arms. She noted the enormous size of the two Norfolk pine trees at the southwest corner of the yard. These trees were only two feet tall when their father had helped her and Aimee Sue plant them. She was thankful they had survived the tornado. Cherished memories from the past flowed through her mind as if they were only yesterday. Thoughts of Aaron, her mother, Aimee as her old bubbly self, and sweet, precious Joey came to her mind. "It's strange," she thought. "Everything keeps changing, the people, the circumstances, but not

Alfaland. It stays the same." The view remained as it had when Kendra was four years old. It seemed to always be there and somehow give her its strength. Alfaland she felt somehow drew her closer to God and truth. She would never speak it, but admitted to herself that she would always love Joey Dubious.

Kendra took several minutes to gain her composure, then picked up the phone and called Joey at the office.

When he answered the phone she began. "Joey, your song..." she hesitated. "It is the most beautiful that I've ever heard."

"Kendra, you heard it, huh? So, you like it?"

"It's beautiful Joey, I'm so proud of you.

"I'm glad you like it," Joey said.

"Did you write that?" She struggled to hide the emotions that were stirring inside her.

"Quite a while ago," he said. He remembered that he'd wrote it the night of her father's wedding.

"When did you record it?"

"We were just fooling around when I was in Nashville on vacation. I hadn't heard anything until a month ago. My buddy, and now my agent," he added, "Jimmy, phoned me and said it was being released and doing well in the south. We recorded an entire CD. I'll give you one."

"I'd love it. I'm really happy for you, Joey." She hesitated a moment, "I suppose this means you'll be leaving?"

"I was going to talk to you about that when you got back. Jimmy's lined us up with a bunch of public appearances after the first of the year. Well, actually New Year's Eve we are going to be in Atlanta. Can you imagine?" He laughed. "I get nervous just thinking about it. The thought petrifies me, to be honest." He hesitated a moment. "What really bothers me is to leave you." He stuttered. "The business and all, I mean."

"I wouldn't think of holding you back, Joey." Kendra said. "You've got too much to offer and to gain. You're a very gifted and special person, Joey. I've always thought that."

"I'm not sure I want to make a lifetime vocation out of this new career, but I'm excited and will enjoy trying it for a few years and see what happens."

He stayed with the *Fort Akers Gazette* until Kendra returned after Thanksgiving. The juggling of his music career and his duties at the paper became difficult.

Kendra arranged a large going away party for Joey. All operations for the afternoon had been closed down.

"It is evident that your life is about to head down a new road, Joey." Kendra stood before the crowd of employees surrounding Joey.

"Your popularity has exploded almost overnight," a worker said. "You're a star, Joey."

"I guess I have no choice but to grab and hang on," Joey said.

"We know you've always been a little shy, Joey, and you don't really enjoy crowds so this is going to be quite a challenge for you," another employee commented.

"That's true." Joey brushed some cake crumbs off his mustache. "I am basically a loner and I have mixed feelings about all the notoriety." Joey grinned, "Although I do love to sing. Once I start singing a lot of the fear goes away."

Lots of hugs, laughter, and tears were exchanged that afternoon. Joey had developed a close bond with the employees over the past several years. They were proud of him, but on the other hand hated to see him leave.

"I promise I'll come back and visit you often," Joey said.

"He'll soon be drawn into a world far different than the one he has here in small town Fort Akers," Kendra thought. "I hope life will be good to him." She wondered what ever happened with him and Julie? He never mentioned her. "One thing I know for sure is that I'm going to miss my sweet friend."

Chapter Fifteen

Two family traditions were brought into play that first winter at Alfaland.
The pond had frozen over early. It was the third week in December and at least six inches of snow were already on the ground making it an ideal Saturday for the first annual Fort Akers Co. *Gazette* Christmas party. Their were laughs, and gasps for breath, as employees and their children skated on the ice, rode toboggan's, inner tubes, and sleds down the hill to the pond. All the while, they were being entertained by Christmas music blaring out into the frigid air.
The following morning, the Bradley's began their family tradition of cutting their own Christmas tree, which turned out to be a hilarious disaster, when Jared didn't get out from under the tree fast enough, and it fell on him. After gaining his composure, a snow ball fight ensued, between Jared and Kendra, before they tied the tree to the sleigh and the three, Jared, Kendra and Ian, strapped in has car seat, pulled it to the house. Aimee Leigh was too little that first year.

Years passed and life continued to generate countless treasured memories for the Bradley family. Present, but absent from the life going on round about her, Aimee Sue remained in a coma. Jared Jr. with blond curly hair and blue eyes entered into their world two years after Aimee Leigh was born.

Ian was a gentle child. Kendra and Jared often described him as an adult in a child's body. He was serious-minded and could be content to entertain himself, whether it be collecting or creating things, for hours at a time. He enjoyed hanging around with adults more than other children. Aimee Leigh, on the other hand, was just the opposite. She was into everything and rarely seemed to grow tired. Aimee was round faced, slightly chubby, and had freckles that popped out in the sun just like her mother's. Aimee was also very much a daddy's girl. Jared Jr. was somewhat of a mixture of the other two.

Kendra had hired enough management at the *Gazette* so that she could spend more time at home, which is what she desired at this point in her life. She wanted to be free to enjoy the children while they were growing up. Her heart just wasn't into a newspaper career.

Joey Dubois did become famous but, unlike his promise, he did not return to Fort Akers.

It was nearing the end of summer and Kendra had spent the afternoon by the pool with Carmon and her, Carmon's, new baby girl. Jared, still in his uniform, joined Kendra at the round picnic table by the pool after working the day shift at the police department.

"Sweetheart, what do you think about the fact that Ian has been calling us Mom and Dad?" Kendra asked. "I thought before the kids get back home we should talk about it and decide." Byron and Jane had taken the three children camping with them in their motor home for a week in Brown County. "It makes me a little uneasy."

Jared stood and reached up to tilt the umbrella in order to block the sun that was hitting him in the face. "I know. I've noticed that he's started doing that the last couple of months." He sat back down in the lawn chair beside the table. "It would be difficult to tell him not to when the other two are."

"I'm sure that's why he's started doing it." Kendra took a sip of her iced tea. "To be honest," she said, "I have a hard time realizing that he's not ours sometimes."

"I do too," Jared said, "I love him, as my own as I know you do, to. I wish we could just adopt him, but, like your folks said, that could get pretty complicated." He shook his head and shrugged his shoulders. "I guess they are right, but I'd like for him to have my last name."

"Me too," Kendra said. "He is such a good kid. It's hard to believe that he'll be going to the first grade next week." She shook her head in disbelief. "And Aimee Leigh will be in kindergarten."

"I think, for Ian's sake, it would be best to just let it be." Jared turned his head and looked at her. "We sure don't want to hurt him. Besides, who knows if Aimee is ever going to come out of her coma? We all have to go on living." He smiled. "I feel we have to think of him first."

"I know you're right. It's just hard not to feel like I'm stealing Aimee's son somehow." Kendra stood up, walked over, and then kissed him. She wrapped her arms around his head, held him to her bikini-clad chest, and then rubbed her hand over his back. "It's good to have you home. Did you have a good day?"

He rubbed his nose over her freckled upper chest and neck. "You smell like coconuts. You look really incredible in that swim suit." He patted her gently on the rear. "My day was great." He smiled. "The chief talked to me today."

"Oh, is that good or bad?" She stroked his forehead.

"Good." Jared raised his eyebrows. "Would you believe he's making me his assistant chief?" he asked.

"Jared, that's great." She leaned over and hugged him. "He apparently thinks very highly of you. Didn't I tell you you're a good officer? Congratulations." She kissed the top of his head. "I'm not surprised."

Jared smiled. "It just has to be approved by the board."

Kendra strolled back down the steps, into the pool, and slipped onto the plastic float on which she had been sunbathing. "Sarah and

Judy had Aimee outside in the sun for a little while this afternoon. They are so good with her. We'd never have survived without those two angels."

"They are a godsend," Jared said. He leaned over, placed his elbows on his knees and his hands under his chin, appreciating the exhibit of her body. He changed the subject knowing discussing Aimee made her sad. "So did you have a good afternoon with Carmon?"

"Fantastic. Her little girl, Sheri, is adorable. She and Charlie are so happy and Carmon gets along great with the boys." Kendra paddled over to the edge of the pool and sat up straddling the plastic float. She balanced herself by hanging onto the edge of the pool with her hands.

Jared bent over and gave her a kiss. "I'm going to go in and change and join you for a swim before dinner. You know, you get sexier with age." She grinned and lay back on the float. He stood up and lingered for a moment, admiring her slim tan body in the skimpy swimsuit. "Hopefully," he said, "we'll be able to spend the entire evening together."

As soon as Jared left and went into the house, Kendra jumped out of the pool and picked up the magazine that Carmon had left for her to read and slipped it into her bag. It was a movie magazine with Joey and some sizzling beauty queen on the front cover. He had made his first movie and was all over the news and tabloids. As far as Kendra knew, he still was not married, but whenever she saw his picture in a magazine he had on a cowboy hat and had some flashy beauty on his arm. At first he had phoned either her or the paper about every six months, but, she hadn't heard from him for over two years.

Chapter Sixteen

It started on Tuesday when Kendra dropped Ian and Aimee Leigh off for their first day of school. She felt melancholy while driving back home.

"What's a matter with me?" Kendra asked herself. Her own feelings took her by surprise. "They're just growing up so fast and I enjoyed them being little." At least she still had little Jared Jr., she said to herself, "for a few more years anyway." She struggled to combat it, but a lump came to her throat and tears to her eyes several times during the short drive back to Alfaland.

The second day went a little easier. No tears were shed. She had just walked in the door from delivering Ian and Aimee Leigh to school and was in the process of removing Jared's coat when the phone rang.

"Mrs. Bradley, I mean Aimee?" The man's voice was loud and harsh coming across the receiver.

"Yes, this is Kendra Bradley." She emphasized her name.

"Kendra, oh yeah," he said. "How ya doing?" He appeared to be groping for something to say.

"Who is this?" Kendra asked. She was a bit irritated.

"I'm an old buddy of your husband, Jared," he said. "Is he there?"

Kendra could hear his heavy breathing. "He can't come to the phone right now." She didn't feel comfortable telling him Jared wasn't home. "Can I give him a message?"

"Just tell him I'd like to talk to him."

"Who shall I say is calling?"

"He'll know!"…He had hung up.

Kendra felt uneasy. "Maybe it's one of those low life's that Jared has to deal with at the department," she thought. "Maybe someone with a grudge, but why did he say Aimee?"

Later that evening, after the kids were asleep and Sarah and Judy were upstairs, Kendra and Jared were alone in the living room on the sofa. Jared had his feet up on the ottoman and Kendra was lying with her head on his lap. The news and weather had just gone off.

"Oh, I just remembered." She sat up. "I had a really strange phone call this morning. It sounded like some grumpy old man. At first he called me Aimee, and then he asked for you." She noticed Jared tense up. "All he said was to tell you he called and you'd know who it is. Who was it? Do you know?"

Jared sat in silence, an angry expression on his face. She'd never seen him look like this before.

Jared made a feeble attempt at a casual response. "It's probably that old drunk. I had to get pretty tough with him the other week."

"But, I don't understand. Why would he call me Aimee instead of Kendra?"

"I don't know." Jared appeared agitated. "Maybe he saw Aimee's baby announcement in the paper or something and got confused. The guy is crazy."

"But that was several years ago?" she asked.

"I don't know, don't worry about it, and if he ever calls again hang up immediately. Don't listen to him. Like I said he's crazy."

"So you know who it is?"

He was quiet again and didn't answer.

"Jared, do you know who it is?" Her voice quivered.

"I know who it is." He pointed his finger at her. "And if the bastard ever calls here again, I'll kill the son of a bitch."

"Jared, what is it? I've never seen you like this."

"Forget it."

"Forget it? Jared who is he?" Fear flooded through her body.

"Forget it; I said I'll take care of it," he said. "I'm going to bed." He left the room.

In shock and bewilderment, Kendra sat motionless for several minutes. Kendra had never seen Jared this upset. She knew in her gut that something was wrong, but she didn't know what to do. When she went to bed his back was turned. Kendra sensed he was pretending to be asleep.

The next morning, Jared got up and dressed for work pretending as if nothing had happened, but there was something different. Kendra wanted to ask him about the night before, but was hesitant. She didn't want to set him off again. He kissed her good-bye; then he hesitated and stepped back, placing his hands on her shoulders and looking into her eyes, not saying a word. Then, almost in a violent manner, he pulled her against him and held her in his arms. Somewhere in the depths of her soul, Kendra knew their utopia had ended. Jared turned and left for work.

The days that followed brought sadness to Kendra's heart as she watched Jared become more and more distant. He bought alcohol, which they never even had in the house before. The minute he got off work he would fix a drink. He would toss and turn all night in bed. Whenever the phone rang, he would grow tense. He spent much of his time outside and in the barn. Worst of all, besides not conversing with Kendra, he ignored the children.

She needed to talk to someone. Kendra called Carmon and made arrangements to meet for lunch.

"I want the old light-hearted, fun-loving Jared back. Where is he?" Kendra lifted her arms in disbelief. "What's happening?" She looked around the restaurant to make sure no one was within hearing distance and then turned her eyes back across the booth to Carmon. "I know it all began with that phone call I received a couple of months ago."

"Is that the only phone call you've received?" Carmon asked.

Kendra nodded and took a bite of her salad. "It seemed for a while like things were getting a little better, but Jared has been drinking a lot more than usual. Almost every night, he makes a drink before going to bed. Sometimes he has two or three drinks and he gets irritated so easy." She shook her head in disbelief. "He never used to do that. He very rarely ever drank at all. He's just not himself anymore." Kendra had to fight back the tears. "Carmon, what am I going to do?"

"I have to agree, my friend, there is definitely something wrong." Carmon motioned to the waitress for a refill of coffee. "Do you have any idea what it is?" she asked after the waitress had left.

"I think about it continually. Is he being threatened? If so, why? Is there another woman? Has he done some terrible thing?" She leaned forward over the table and whispered. "But I know he loves me, Carmon. I just can't believe that there is anyone else."

"Have you tried to talk to him about it?"

"Not since that first night." Kendra shook her head, "I may have been wrong, but I've had the feeling that, whatever it is, he's trying to erase it from his life. I thought maybe the best way to help him would be by not bringing it up. Does that make any sense?"

"Well, it would, but things don't seem to be getting any better by not facing whatever it is. Are they?"

"No, something's destroying him. Some ominous black cloud is looming over our lives Carmon, and I feel helpless to do anything about it. Even our lovemaking has changed." She hesitated. "Until last night." She wasn't going to mention it, but she had to tell someone. It was too much of a weight to carry alone. Kendra glanced around the room then put her hand up to the side of her mouth and spoke in a near whisper. "In the middle of our lovemaking, he just stopped and started crying uncontrollably. He's falling apart, Carmon. He cried on my shoulder like a child. He's hurting so bad."

"What did you do?"

"I just held him, stroking his head and kissing him. I didn't say a word, other than to tell him I loved him."

"I can't believe you didn't say anything," Carmon said. "I couldn't have kept my mouth shut."

"I don't know." Kendra shrugged. "Maybe I'm afraid to know what it is. He finally fell off to sleep." Kendra laid her hands on the table, "I realized last night that I couldn't let this go on any longer and I told him that this morning."

Carmon wiped her mouth with her napkin. "What did he say?"

"To my surprise, he agreed. He asked me to give him today. He wanted talk to the chief about getting some time off and he said he would tell me the entire story tonight."

"No wonder you're a nervous wreck today." Carmon reached over and touched Kendra's hand.

Kendra had to leave to go pick up Aimee at kindergarten. "Thanks for listening," she said as they both got in their cars to leave. "You're a dear friend. I don't know what I'd do without you."

"I just wish I could be more help." Carmon pulled the door shut and spoke out the window. "Will you let me know how things turn out?"

Kendra nodded and sighed. "I'll call you tomorrow."

While driving to school she recalled Jared's words when he had kissed her good-bye that morning.

"I'll tell you the whole story after today. Just let me say this. It's not you, Kendra. I love you and the kids more than I love myself and I don't want to do anything to hurt you." He had placed his hands on her shoulders. "Do you know that?" he asked. "Do you believe that?"

She had nodded. He'd had tears in his eyes. So had she.

"I'll stand by you, no matter what," she had said.

Jared had, for a brief moment, appeared like his old self. He stared into her eyes and whispered, "I love you, I'll always love you." He kissed her with more passion than he had in several weeks.

When Jared drove off in his squad car that morning, she had felt apprehensive. She felt like maybe she should have gone with him. "No," she said to herself. "Whatever this is, I've got to let him take care of it in the way he thinks best."

He wasn't home and it was past dinnertime. Sarah had prepared chili, so the family went ahead and ate, but Kendra had a hard time eating anything. Sarah and Judy were aware that something was wrong. They had known it for quite some time.

"We'll go ahead and bath the kids and put them to bed." Sarah said.

"Thanks," Kendra said. "I'd appreciate it."

They didn't ask any questions, which Kendra appreciated.

Kendra waited. She tried to watch television but she couldn't concentrate on anything. She could not sit still. She walked through the house, wringing her hands. She waited until eight o'clock and then decided to phone the chief. "First, though," she thought. "Maybe I should call the department and see if Jared may still be there." She couldn't stand waiting any longer. She had to do something. She was going crazy. "What was he doing? Why didn't he come home?" The dispatcher answered after two rings. Kendra made a feeble attempt to be light hearted and casual. "Is Jared Bradley still working?"

"He's not on duty right now," the dispatcher said. "Could another officer help you?"

"No," Kendra said. "This is Kendra Bradley. Do you know when he left?"

"Oh, hello, Mrs. Bradley…Well he went off duty at five-thirty, but I think he left with the chief. They didn't exactly say what they were doing. I'm not sure if they were working on a case or what?"

Kendra thanked her and hung up the phone.

"Now what?" She thought. She didn't know much more than before. "What was he doing? Maybe he was talking to Chief Troyer about whatever is bothering him."

Kendra poured herself a cup of coffee, walked out on the porch, and then sat down at the wicker table. She could see out to the road. She spotted lights coming up the drive. She hurried to the back door!

Her heart sank when she opened the door. She could see that it wasn't his car. She strained to see under the dim light in the yard. It was an older man she'd never seen before. He had on a large bulky coat and a black stocking hat with thick shaggy, grayish brown hair protruding out from the side. He appeared as if he hadn't bathed in weeks. She didn't feel like talking to anyone but she couldn't go back in. He'd already seen her.

He walked stiffly up toward the door where she was standing, still holding the door open.

"Mrs. Bradley?" he asked in a harsh, husky voice. She knew his voice from the phone conversation. He carried a small manila envelope in his right hand.

"Who are you? What do you want?" Kendra found herself yelling at the old man. "Get out of here. My husband doesn't want you here." She hated this man and she didn't even know who he was. All she knew was that he was the center of all the hurt and pain she had suffered for the past couple months. He was evil, maybe, she felt, even the devil himself.

"He's forced me to do this, Mrs. Bradley." His voice softened. "You are a pretty lady. He thinks he's going to buffalo me." He became harsh. "Well, he's not." He reached out his hand with the envelope. "These are for you."

Keeping her eyes on the stranger, Kendra reached out her hand and grabbed the envelope without even looking at it. She believed this was something she must do in order to put an end to this nightmare. Maybe she'd burn whatever it is and not even look at it.

Kendra heard a noise come from the northwest corner of the house. Someone was in the shadows. Her knees grew weak. She trembled! The figure walked out into the light. It was Jared, holding his gun with both hands stretched out in front of him and pointed at the old man.

Jared kept the gun aimed at the man and with his left hand pulled his radio from his belt. He put it up to his mouth. "I got him, chief."

"Where are you?" She heard the response come back over the radio.

"Now, turn around, slowly with your hands in the air and back towards me," Jared ordered the man.

The man did not move.

"Do it now," Jared said, "or I'll blow your brains out, you son of a bitch."

"Jared, what's your 10-20?" Chief Troyer's voice shouted over the radio. "Jared where are you?"

The old man did as he was ordered. "Your lovely wife's gonna know you were fucking her pretty little sister," he said as he turned around, "and that the little bastard she has is yours. You don't screw with me, Bradley. You think you're so high and mighty. All you had to do was help me out a little, but no, you want to keep all your wife's money for yourself."

"Shut up! Shut up!" Jared yelled.

"What ya gonna do?" he snarled. "Shoot me in front of your lovely lady here? She ain't ever gonna want your body in her bed again."

Screaming in disgust, Kendra turned toward the old man. "You animal! Your plan won't work." Her entire body shivered. "I'd never leave Jared no matter what."

"You don't need to answer this piece of scum, Kendra," Jared said while continuing to hold the gun at the man's back. Jared's voice was resolute, yet tender. "He's not worth acknowledging."

"What's he doing?" Kendra saw the old man was turning around and digging into his pants." Before she could speak or comprehend what was happening, an explosion of gunfire erupted.

"Get down!" Jared shouted before falling backwards.

Crippled with fear, Kendra fell to the cold ground near the porch.

Again, gunfire blasted the night air.

A dead silence consumed the darkness. Jared lay on his side on the sidewalk in front of the porch with his legs in the grass. Blood covered the front of his uniform and the sidewalk beneath him. His hat and gun lay on the ground in front of him. Shaking and sobbing, Kendra crawled on her hands and knees over the damp grass toward him. Jared turned his head, focusing on her with pain filled eyes.

Jared reached out his hand toward her. "Kendra, I'm sorry," he said. His face was splattered with blood. She grabbed his arm and held his hand to her cheek sobbing.

"Hang on, sweetheart," she pleaded. She spotted the police radio on the ground, grabbed it, and then pressed the only button she could find. "Send help quickly! Jared Bradley's been shot!" She said between sobs. "Help...Please, hurry! Help! Is anybody there?"

"I hear you Mrs. Bradley!" The dispatcher's voice came over the radio. It was the same one she had spoke to earlier. "What's your location?"

"At home. We're at home," Kendra shouted. "Please hurry!"

"We will hurry, Mrs. Bradley."

"Hang on. "Mrs. Bradley is the suspect still there?"

Kendra had forgotten all about him. She looked around. She could see the old man was on the ground.

She placed the radio to her mouth again. "I think there was just one," she said, her voice quivering. "He has been shot but, I think he's dead. He's not moving."

Kendra saw Jared's eyes were focusing behind her. She turned and her heart sank. Ian stood near the steps in his robe and slippers.

"Daddy," little Ian's voice cried out. "Daddy, are you okay?" He ran over and fell on his knees beside Jared. Kendra didn't pull him back. She hated for him to see this, but somehow she knew she couldn't intervene. This was far too important to them.

"I'll be okay, son," Jared put his hand behind Ian's neck. "I love you, son," he whispered. "You are going to need to be strong, son." Jared displayed a meager smile. "You know I'm proud of you." Ian nodded. Jared stroked the front of Ian's robe. "You are going to need to be my big boy and help take care of your mother for me."

"I will, Daddy," Ian said.

Tears flowed down Kendra's face. "Honey, hold on," she said. "Help's coming. You can make it. We'll be all right, please hang on. I love you. Remember you promised you'd never leave me, honey?"

Kendra was hysterical when she felt a hand touch her shoulder. Judy and Sarah were behind them. Jared's blood continued to cover the ground and sidewalk. Sarah gently pulled Ian to his feet.

The chief and the ambulance arrived moments before state, city and county officers flooded the property. The suspect was found to be dead.

The medics loaded Jared onto a stretcher and up into the

ambulance. Kendra, still on her knees, turned to Ian and, with shaking hands, slipped the manila envelope to him. "Hide this somewhere if you can," she said, "and don't let anyone see it." She put her arms around him, holding him for a moment and stroking the back of his head before joining Jared in the ambulance. "Mommy will call you just as soon as I know anything."

The little boy slipped the envelope under his robe and took it into the house. Kendra left in the ambulance with Jared. It broke her heart that he had to go through this night. She was going to make sure he had his daddy's name someday. It was a name to be proud of.

Jared was unconscious by the time they left in the ambulance and he was wheeled into surgery when they reached the hospital.

While Kendra was in the waiting room, Lori Bradley, Carmon, Charlie and every officer from the department, both on and off-duty, and many of their wives joined her. Officers from Elkhart Co. came to the Fort Akers Police Dept. and took over for the officers so they could stay at the hospital. The chief and many of the officer's prayed with her. Several of the officers called their pastors and had them put out prayer chains to their congregations for the Bradley family. It was special to see the unique brotherly bond that emerged between the officers during moments like this.

Lori was devastated. This was the second time she'd lived this nightmare. Jared was her pride and joy, her only child.

In less than an hour several doctors, including Dr. Scott, appeared in the waiting room with the news. "There was nothing more we could do. Jared didn't make it." A gasp echoed through the room. Dr. Scott glanced down at the floor, and then back up again. "He was hit four times in various areas of the body and, even though he had on his bullet proof vest, he just lost too much blood." He looked at Kendra. "I'm so sorry."

The memory of the earlier scene at Alfaland and the words that the ugly man had spoken were locked in the back of Kendra's mind.

There was one more thing that needed to be completed before she could allow herself to mourn. She asked Dr. Scott if she could speak to him alone. Dr. Scott nodded and led her to his hospital office.

Kendra took hold of his hands as soon as the door closed. "Doc, I'm not out of my mind. I have to ask you to do something right away and not ask me any questions. Please. I don't know what you need to do, but if you need a blood test, or whatever, so we have the information we need to…" she yelled, "To verify that Ian is Jared's son. He would want this, please. Is there anyway this can be done?" They would both want this."

Dr. Scott was speechless for a moment, then said. "I see." He withheld a strong desire to question her. He nodded. "I understand. I'll take care of it." Without a word he wrapped his arms around her. "I'm so sorry you have to live through this pain again Kendra. I can call your father for you, if you want."

"Thanks, if you would, I would appreciate it." She left the room knowing the days ahead were going to be rough, but ones she must face.

The following morning the chief of police came to Alfaland to speak with Kendra about what had happened the night before.

"Before you say anything," Chief Troyer said, "Jared had reported to me that there was apparently an attempted blackmail going on. The question is, and I need for you to be honest about this, was the department involved or could the department be harmed in any way by whatever they had on him? Was he selling drugs, or stealing, or anything of that nature? Or, was it something personal that did not involve the police department?"

Kendra looked up at him with bloodshot eyes. "I swear, it was not related to his occupation or department in any way. It was between him and me and it…it definitely wasn't worth dying over." She fought back the tears.

"Apparently," the chief said, "this guy thought he'd found a gold mine. The old man was a short-term employee of the P.I. firm that Jared used to work for. He was fired from there some time ago for dishonest practices. He lived in Indianapolis and was into several illegal activities. He had two warrants out on him." He placed his hands on his knees. "That's all I need to know." He picked up his hat that was on the sofa beside him. "Except for one more question." His eyes met hers. "Can you verify who shot first?"

"It was the old man," she said.

"That's all I needed to know. As far as whatever this was about, I will not make that any of my concern and it won't be mentioned again by me, if you prefer."

"I prefer," Kendra said. "Thank you."

"Jared was a good officer, a friend, and very highly thought of. We consider him killed in the line of duty. He was attempting to uphold the law over his own personal needs and safety. My report to the newspapers will read that he encountered a suspicious subject at his residence. When he attempted to confront the man, he was shot and wounded but was able to take down the suspect. He later died as a result of his injuries. I'd advise you though." He paused. "To prepare yourself for questions, being who you are and all. It might be a good idea to have your story together ahead of time, if you understand what I mean?"

"Thanks, chief, I understand." She shook his hand. "I do understand what you're saying. I'll do that. I'll prepare myself."

Chief Troyer left the room.

"God forgive me," Kendra thought to herself, "I don't know who shot first." She lowered her head for a moment. She didn't want a lengthy investigation. That settled it in Kendra's mind. She did what she had to do. Her family came first. She would never speak of it again.

The funeral of assistant chief, Jared Lyndon Bradley, was one that the residents in the small community of Fort Akers, Indiana would hold in their memories for many years to come. The viewers watched in silent admiration as a parade of over two hundred city, county and state police cars drove through the city in honor of their fallen comrade. The procession drove past the police department then continued through Fort Akers and out to the secluded cemetery where Jared would be laid to rest, only two miles from the home he so dearly loved, Alfaland.

Kendra sat in the center seat of the limousine with Jared Jr. and Aimee Leigh on each side of her. Mr. Patton, Jane, and Ian were in the seat behind them. Kendra's eyes focused on the black hearse, with two small American flags fluttering on each rear fender, gliding down the road before them. Kendra felt the pain of two deaths, Jared's, and second the death of the truth upon which their relationship had been built. She wasn't even sure what that truth was. And the most difficult fact to face was that she would probably never know.

She recalled the previous morning when she had a chance to take Ian aside. Kneeling down before him, she had asked, "Sweetheart, did you hide the envelope?"

"Yes." He took her hand and led her up the stairs, through the main bath, to the third floor. Kendra had been surprised that he was even aware the room existed. He showed her a large crack in the wall where he had stuck the envelope. It was not visible, but she was able to reach it with her fingers.

"Did you look inside?" she asked.

Ian nodded and lowered his head.

Kendra's heart sank. She regretted forcing him into the middle of this as.

As if to relieve her curiosity, Ian said, "It's pictures of Dad and my other mommy, Aimee."

Kendra suppressed the agony that pierced her soul. "Pretty cool, huh? Daddy is really, daddy! Do you understand that, Ian? He loved you so much. And, we love him and both know he had his reasons for not telling us the story. He loved you so much."

"I know," he looked up at her and said, "I just wish you were my mom, though."

She knelt down in front of him and held his hands, "Ian, sometimes certain people in life have a special bond. That's the way it is with you and I. Even if we were not related at all, I'd love you. And..." she affectionately stroked his curly head. "I'll tell you something else. You would love your mommy, Aimee, too, if you knew her as I have and, who knows, maybe someday you will."

"She's pretty!" he said. "She looks so much better in those pictures."

Kendra drew from within herself an inner strength and pulled the pictures out of the wall and opened the envelope. Sadness overcame her as her eyes fell upon the smiling young Jared with his arms around her sister. It appeared as if they were at a party somewhere. There was even a picture of them kissing. She looked at each one of them and then passed them to Ian. Kendra couldn't bear to look at them any longer.

"They are beautiful pictures, aren't they Ian?" She stroked his hair again. "That's the way your mother use to look before she got hurt. Let's just put them back here in the wall." Kendra smiled at the precious child she so dearly loved. "This will be our little secret. Sometime in the future, Ian, you will probably want to change your last name to your daddy's name, but it would be hard to explain this right now. Can you understand? It would make some people think badly of Daddy. I will help you when the time comes, but these are your pictures to keep, okay?"

There was a noise at the bottom of the stairway. "Kendra, are you up here? Are you all right?" It was Lori Bradley.

"Ian," Kendra whispered, "let's tell Lori our little secret. She would be so happy to know that you are her grandson, too! I think your daddy would want us to tell her."

Ian nodded in excitement. He liked Lori, and he was proud to tell someone what, to him, was so special. He had a father, and it was the one man in his life that he most loved.

"Tell you what," Kendra said. I need to go down with the others. I'll tell Lori to come up here, that we have a secret for her, and you can show her the pictures, okay?" Kendra had to leave. She didn't want to see the pictures again.

"Okay." Ian nodded and smiled.

Kendra got up and went to meet Lori at the bottom of the steps. The two women embraced, sharing their mutual sorrow.

"Ian has something pretty special he wants to show you upstairs," Kendra said. "I ask you to please just keep it to yourself for now." She took Lori's hand in hers. "We'll talk about it later. It's a little secret we are going to share with you. I think you'll understand after you talk with Ian."

Lori had gone on up the stairs and Kendra headed down to fellowship with the others that were gathered at Alfaland.

Now, in the limousine on the drive to the cemetery, Kendra gazed out over the partially husked cornfields and noted the trees with their multi-colors. Kendra thought, "By talking to Ian yesterday, I believe I was able to help him through this. The fact that he knows he has a father, and it is Jared, even in his sorrow; he feels good about himself. He has an identity that he is proud of. At least the evil man wasn't the complete winner in all this. I just wonder so much…Jared; I wish you were here to explain."

The huge parade of vehicles neared their destination, and Kendra's eyes began to fill with tears. The hearse, followed by the two limousines, turned onto the dirt drive and into the cemetery, followed by the endless train of police cars.

The words from the pastor's message kept going over and over in her mind. "Death," he had said, "will be swallowed up in victory." Kendra believed that. She found consolation in those words. In her heart she knew she and the kids would be all right.

Chapter Seventeen

"There are things," Lori Bradley said, "that make more sense to me now that I know about Ian." She finished folding a pair of Jared's designer jeans and laid them in a box on the bed. She was spending the day helping Kendra sort through Jared's clothes and personal belongings. She sat down on the edge of the bed and looked around the room. "There were times, I can see, when Jared dropped small hints, but…" She shook her head several times. "Who'd have ever imagined?" She thought for a moment. "I do know he really wanted to adopt Ian." She looked at Kendra. "He mentioned that several times."

"I know he did," Kendra said. "I can recall some things he said, too, that I didn't understand at the time." Kendra slid a couple of paper sacks to the side and found an empty spot on the bed, which was covered with Jared's personal belongings stacked in neat piles and boxes to give to different individuals, and sat down also. Several police uniforms were hanging on the back of the bedroom door. Kendra looked around the room. "It's so hard for me to let go of any of his things." She glanced at the picture of Jared on the dresser in his police uniform.

"I know," Lori said. "Believe me, I understand." She looked toward the ceiling while she fought back tears. "It's all so final." She crossed her legs and folded her arms on her lap. "One thing I've wanted to say, Kendra." She looked at her daughter in law. "What you did and how you've handled this is the most precious and unselfish action I have ever seen. It is clear why my son loved you so, and..." she added, "I know he did love you. We'll probably never have the complete answer, not in this life anyway, as to why he did what he did but, please..." She reached over and laid her hand over Kendra's knee. "Don't ever doubt for a moment that Jared loved you. He would have been so proud of you and, for him and Ian, I want to say, thank you. Thank you from the bottom of my heart. If there is ever anything I can do to help, I'm here. I love you."

"Thanks, I need you to be here." Kendra placed her hand over Lori's. "I never thought I'd go through this a second time. At least this time I have the children. They mean the world to me. That's what my life is going to consist of now, Lori, my children." She jumped up and headed back to the closet where she had been working. "I think too I may become more active at the *Gazette* again." She picked up a paper sack, got down on her hands and knees and carefully began to place Jared's shoes in it. "I have to keep busy or I'll go crazy. I do know one thing though." She stopped for a moment and looked at Lori. "I'm never going to get married again. I've had love and lost it twice. I never want to go through this again."

"There is one more thing; I want to talk to you about." Lori said. "I think it is important for you to tell your family the truth. They deserve to know, Kendra. Why, don't you tell them? If they find out some other way, it could be much worse."

Kendra was silent for a moment then said, "Lori, I can't right now. I just can't get the words out. Besides that, everybody has had to adjust to so much; I don't want to dump this on them. I will, just give me some time."

"It's a lot to expect out of Ian, too," Lori said.

"I know, Lori. I love that boy so much. He's so wise for his age. I hate it so, that he had to be there when Jared got shot."

"Will you just think about it?" Lori asked.

"Yes, I have been, Lori, and I will." Kendra promised.

Ian made the request a few weeks after the funeral, "Mom, would it be possible for me to have my bedroom on the third floor?" He'd had a special drawing to that room, and Kendra understood. She agreed it was a good idea to have a room all his own. A few days later she found he had hung several pictures and posters around in the room. "This is good for him," she thought. "He definitely has plenty of space here to work with. This will help him. It's good to occupy his mind with something." Just out of curiosity, she checked to find the envelope still stuck in the wall where they had left it. "I'm thankful he hasn't mentioned it. I know I am going to have to tell Dad and Jane sometime, but not yet. I just can't."

To her shame, it took several days after Jared's death before Kendra had the strength to enter into Aimee's room. She stood beside Aimee's bed and stared into her younger sister's frail face. "I feel so guilty," she thought. "I feel jealous. The thought of him loving you makes me ill. I feel guilty because I feel jealous. My mind keeps churning with endless questions and uncontrollable emotions. Did he love you like he loved me? Did he say the things to you that he said to me? Did he touch you like he touched me? I hate it! How can I live with this?" she thought. "I can understand why Jared had been so torn up inside. I wonder if he ever came in here to see you. How did he live with himself? What if you would have come out of your coma? How could he have done this? Oh, Aimee," she sighed. "What have I done? I pray to God that this will never come between us."

Kendra sat down on a vinyl chair beside the bed. She took Aimee's hand and held it in hers.

"I remember," Kendra said, "that day over seven years ago when we took you to the university for the first time. It was your first experience away from home." Kendra lifted Aimee's hand and held it to her cheek. "You were apprehensive and excited. I remember how you came into my bedroom that night before you left for school and the lengthy discussion we had concerning life and our future plans. Remember, Aimee?" she asked. "I was engaged to Aaron at that time and was going to move out myself soon. It was a momentous time for us." Kendra smiled and sighed. "To say goodbye to our secure and happy childhood and step out into the unknown world. We had so much. How did we end up here...?"

Aimee Sue flourished in college. She was actively involved with everything she possibly could be that first year. She kept physically active on the swim team but her favorite activity was the drama club. Aimee had an outstanding voice, and she felt it her highest honor when she was chosen to play the part of Maria in their production of the *Sound of Music*. She managed to stay on the honor roll in spite of her lack of sleep and shabby diet. Aimee was a fun-loving person. Sometimes she could exaggerate, but always knew where to draw the line, and did. She was known as the girl with the permanent smile because of her persistent smile that surrounded her beautiful white teeth, which had just a hint of an overbite.

During the last semester of Aimee's second year at Indiana University, on a Friday night in February, something happened that changed Aimee's life. Carrie, an acquaintance in her social sciences class, invited Aimee to go along with her to a party in Indianapolis that night.

Aimee was a little concerned and surprised when Carrie picked her up. No one else was with them. "I just assumed there were others going," Aimee said when she stepped into the small red Pontiac Sunbird.

"Everybody else has other plans," Carrie said.

"I feel a little uneasy about not driving," Aimee thought. She always liked to drive so she could leave if she wanted. "But, I can't think of any comfortable way to get out of this situation at this point."

The party turned out to be a dud, in Aimee's eyes, but Carrie appeared to be having a terrific time. She'd met a guy, which to Aimee, was offensive. He was rude, loud, used fowl language and was drunk. Carrie began to drink excessively and got drunk also. Aimee was embarrassed to be with her and was regretting the decision to come along.

"I'm going to do the driving back to campus," she thought. "I just have to get the keys away from her."

Aimee noted that there was another person at the party who didn't appear to be happy about being there either. She noticed he had been sitting by himself for quite some time. This handsome man was nursing a beer and intensely involved in shelling peanuts and eating them out of a large basket that was on the table. A hefty pile of shells had already accumulated on his napkin. Aimee couldn't keep her eyes off him. He had shoulder-length blond curly hair, blue eyes that appeared to sparkle, and, a magnificently charming grin." He was wearing a Notre Dame t-shirt with a baggy blue flannel hooded shirt over it.

Aimee concluded he was more interested in the peanuts he was munching on than the futile efforts of a few girls who tried to gain his attention.

Aimee walked over and asked him if he'd like to dance.

He hesitated, looking at her for a moment. "Certainly," he said.

They began to dance. "Are you hungry?" Aimee asked.

"As a matter of fact, I'm starved." He took a step back and looked at her. "How could you tell?" He proceeded to dance. "I neglected to take time for dinner tonight because my, so called, friend, and neighbor, was in such a big hurry to get to this party." He looked around the room. "Now I think he's left with someone. I was considering leaving myself." He grinned, "As soon as I finished that basket of peanuts." They both laughed. He looked into her eyes and smiled. "Somehow you don't seem to fit here in this picture either." He leaned closer to her, raising his eyebrows and lowering his voice. "To tell the truth, I keep waiting for the police to show up. How'd you happen to be here?"

"I came with a friend, or should I say acquaintance, from school. She's really enjoying this. She's also had way too much to drink." Aimee glanced around the room, attempting to locate Carrie. "I don't see her." She stopped dancing and searched the room, becoming more aggravated by the moment. She looked back at him. "This could be serious."

"Was she tall and skinny with straight long black hair and jeans that fit like skin?"

Aimee nodded, feeling somewhat embarrassed. "That's her," she said. "The last I saw her, she was falling all over a guy with weird hair."

He shook his head, "I'm afraid that's my neighbor," he said. "They left together about twenty minutes ago. She must have driven, because he didn't have a car. Besides that, he's suspended."

"Oh great...that is just great. I came with her. That creep," Aimee placed her hands firmly on her hips. "I knew I shouldn't have done this. When I go somewhere I like to drive myself."

"Where did you come from?"

"IU at Bloomington," she answered.

"Oh wow, you are a ways from home."

"Tell me about it. Now what am I going to do?" Aimee was so frustrated she thought she was going to cry.

"Well, I'm not doing anything. If she doesn't come back, I'll drive you home. That would be better than hanging around here. I promise I'm a good driver. Now don't worry," he assured her, "you'll be all right. By the way my name is Jared Bradley."

"Thanks." She struggled to gain her composure. "I'm Aimee Patton."

The party didn't seem quite so bad for either of them now; they danced and talked nonstop. Before they knew it, an hour had gone by.

"It doesn't look like she's coming back," Aimee said when they sat down for a break. "I can't believe she's doing this to me." She tilted her head to one side and raised her eyebrows. "Looks like you're stuck with me, if the offer still stands."

"No problem, as a matter of fact I'm kind of glad she didn't come back." He grinned at her. "I'd rather the evening didn't end so soon now that I've been fortunate enough to have met Cinderella. I'm ready to leave anytime you are."

"I'm ready," she smiled, "If you're sure you want to do this."

"I'm sure," he said. "Let go." He stood.

They located their coats and headed outside.

"Wow," Aimee said when they walked out the door. "The weather's made a dramatic change for the worse while we were inside." She zipped up her coat. "It's cold."

"Looks like we've had several inches of snow," Jared helped Aimee into his Jeep, went around to the other side, and then reached in to start the vehicle. "He got a broom out of the back and swept the snow off the windows. He then got inside. "We'll set here and wait a minute for the heater to begin to blow warmer air."

Aimee was shivering. She was somewhat uneasy concerning this entire situation. Here she was with a total stranger, in unfamiliar surroundings, in the middle of a snowstorm. "How did I manage to get myself into this position?" She asked herself. "I guess I should be thankful that he's willing to drive me home."

"Where are you from, Aimee?" Jared asked.

"Fort Akers, it's in the northern part of the state, close to South Bend. Do you know where that is?"

"You're kidding; South Bend is where I grew up. I've been to Fort Akers. My mother goes down in that area to the Amish Acres art festival every year. She lives in South Bend. My father was a police officer in South Bend."

"You live in Indianapolis now?" she asked.

"Yeah, I work for a public investigating firm in Indy."

After the Jeep had warmed up, Jared found his way to the 465 bypass and turned south on highway 37 heading toward Bloomington. "Unfortunately," Jared said, "It seems the further south we drive the heavier the snow is. I can hardly see six feet ahead."

Traffic began to dwindle and slow to a crawl.

"I can't see," Jared said. "Where's the edge of the road? Now that all the traffic is gone, I don't have any tracks to follow."

"I can't either." Aimee's eyes were glued to the road ahead. "Watch out! There's a car sitting there."

Jared turned the wheel; they slid sideways and just missed the vehicle. He turned the wheel back and they quit sliding. "Whoa that was close. I didn't see it. My eyes are burning; I don't think I'm blinking. I'm staring so hard. "Thanks for your help." He leaned back in the seat and took a deep breath. "What's making this worse now, are all these cars that have pulled off."

"Maybe we should," Aimee said. Her body was shaking but she tried to hide it from Jared. She didn't want to make him more nervous.

"I'd hate to pull off and just set there. Hard telling how bad this may get. We could be stranded for hours. We don't have any water and if we run out of gas we wouldn't have any heat. I'm going to keep moving...where did that car come from?"

"I don't know it just appeared out of no where," Aimee said.

"At least now I have some tracks to follow."

"He's going off the road, Jared." Aimee shouted.

"I see it...hang on." He swerved and pulled back on the road. The car in front of him drove right into a semi that was pulled over.

"Oh god," Aimee said, "What can we do?"

"We can't do anything unless you have a cell phone?"

"No, I didn't bring it. Another dumb thing I did tonight." Do you think we are going to make it?"

"Let's hope."

They drove by another car sitting down in a ravine.

"I think I'll turn my emergency flashers on; looks like everybody else is."

They continued on at a snail's pace for nearly an hour and the traffic dropped off to only an occasional vehicle on the road. The wipers, flopping back and forth, and the heavy snowfall almost caused a hypnotic effect on them.

"This is eerie!" Aimee said her eyes, still glued to the road ahead. "It's almost like we've entered another world and we're the only ones in it."

"I know; it's like we are in the twilight zone. The wind is picking up," Jared said. "If I go any slower we'll be stopped." He quickly looked over at her. "Why don't you turn on the radio?"

Aimee reached over and turned on the radio.

The announcement came over the radio "The national weather

service is advising people to stay off the roads except for extreme emergency. A blizzard warning has been issued for Friday night through Sunday. This is going to be a bad one folks."

"Jared, I am so sorry I got you into this mess," Aimee said. She reached over and touched his shoulder while still keeping her eyes fastened to the road.

"We're in this together, little one," he said smiling even as he stared ahead and gripped the wheel with both hands. He took an anxious deep breath, "I'm sure glad I bought this four wheel drive or we'd have been immobilized an hour ago."

After nearly three tense, stressful hours of crawling through the blowing and drifting snow they finally began to see streetlights and glimpses of buildings through the gusts of snow. "There is practically no traffic on the streets," Jared said by the time they reached Bloomington.

"Everything is at a stand still," the radio announcer said. "The state and county highway crews have been pulled off the roads until further notice and the State Police are closing down the highways."

Jared glanced at her for a second. "I'd say we made it just in time. We're very lucky we made it."

"I think those angels that my mother claims she has watching over me were along tonight." She wrung her hands together. "That was tense," Aimee sighed. She directed Jared to the correct turns in order to find their way to her little apartment near the campus.

Covered with snow and exhausted from their tense experience, they walked into Aimee's apartment. Jared teased, "I'm grateful you've allowed me to come inside, little one." Shivering, they took off their wet coats and placed them on the floor by the door.

"I'm so grateful for you," Aimee said. "Can you imagine how much more of a nightmare this could have been with Carrie driving in her drunken state or even me driving her little car?" She put both her hands to her cheeks. "I shutter to think what could have happened. I owe you, Mr. Bradley."

"I'm glad I was there." Jared smiled at her. "You'd probably be sitting in a ditch somewhere."

"How about if I start by finding you something to eat?" Aimee asked, "I don't have much."

"Hey, anything would be great." He laughed. "Except maybe peanuts."

"Don't worry, not peanuts." She laughed. Aimee made him some hot chocolate and toast while Jared took off his wet boots and socks and placed them near the radiator.

"You know," Jared, admitted, "I had some doubts as to whether we were going to make it." He sipped the hot chocolate, shivering more from nerves than cold.

"You're a good driver, Jared, just like you said." She smiled and took a sip of hot chocolate. "Thank you for getting me home." She paused a moment and looked at him. "I hope you didn't have anything pressing back in Indy, because I think you're stranded here."

"Not really." His lips quivered. "Just another lonely, boring weekend." He smiled. "This is an unusual, but pleasant, switch."

Aimee had grown to feel safe with this man and had no hesitation about him staying there for the night.

Jared ate six pieces of toast and drank two cups of hot chocolate before he finished. Aimee then discovered a bag of Oreo Cookies and they devoured several of those.

"I believe I've finally had enough to eat." Jared leaned back and wrapped up in the comforter she had given him. "It's so comfy here. I like your apartment!"

The wind whistled and roared outside, but they felt warm and secure. The two sat on the sofa each, wrapped in their individual blankets, and talked for several hours revealing their life stories to each other.

Jared told Aimee about his recent divorce from his childhood sweetheart and the struggles he'd been having adjusting to the single life again. "It's hard," he said. "I was just thinking, sitting at the party tonight, how much I hate that life. I guess I like having someone special in my life. I don't like being alone." He looked over at Aimee curled up to her neck in the huge blanket. "Do you believe in fate?" he asked.

She hesitated, "Not until tonight. I haven't really minded being alone, but I've never been in love so maybe I never knew what I was missing. I've never admitted this to anyone..." she hesitated a moment. "But I've never had sex. I know that's unusual, but I've always wanted to wait for Mr. Right to come along. I guess it's my upbringing and family. My parents have something so special, and so does my sister, Kendra. She saved herself for Aaron. They just got married this year and they are so happy. I want that for myself."

They had turned, facing each other with their arms on the back of the sofa. He stared into her brown eyes for a moment. "I'm surprised at your honesty. You are very unique and special." He touched her hand.

Their eyes locked and without words, their bodies drew closer. After a moment of hesitation, uncertain of each other, their lips touched. Refraining for a moment, their eyes met again. Jared ran his fingers through her short dark hair. Their lips met again. This time with no hesitation, followed by a succession of several more kisses, each more lengthy and passionate than the previous. Jared lifted up his blanket and Aimee nestled inside and curled up on his lap as he wrapped both arms and blanket around her. Aimee kissed his ear and neck over and over again. She'd never felt such passion. I'm not sure." Her voice was quivering. "I've never felt this way before." Aimee wrapped her arms around Jared's neck and rested her head on his shoulder. "I hardly know you but yet I feel I've always known you."

"Perhaps fate had a hand in both our lives tonight," Jared said as he kissed her forehead. "I've been so lonely."

They sat in silence, embraced in each other's arms for several moments. Aimee finally broke the silence. "I'm so glad I went tonight," she said.

He squeezed her shoulder. "I am too, little one. This may sound crazy Aimee, but I'm not looking for a one-night stand. I'm looking for more."

"I know that," she said kissing his ear. "I'm willing to gamble that you are my Mr. Right."

Aimee lay with her head on his shoulder and he could sense her crying. He turned and could see tears running down her face. Jared's heart sank. "Aimee what's wrong? Did I say something?"

"There's nothing wrong," she said, wiping her eyes with her fingers. "I feel something I've never felt before. It's wonderful."

"You are the most unique person I've ever met," he said, "and I do understand what you are saying. I'm so glad that I went tonight."

It was after five in the morning. The wind was howling outside and the snow was whipping against the windows when the new lovers fell off to sleep. It had been a strange and wonderful night for both of them. Neither had expected anything so special to happen when the evening had begun.

They were both still wrapped in the blanket on the sofa several hours later when Aimee woke up. The wind outside had died down somewhat, but it was still snowing.

"I feel like a new woman," Aimee thought. She was excited about having Jared there. She slipped out from his arms and made a pot of coffee. She found some cinnamon rolls in the refrigerator and put them in the oven. She then went back to the couch and sat admiring Jared for several minutes as he lay sleeping. She nuzzled up next to him, kissing him and stroking his hair. She loved touching him and being near him.

That fateful weekend turned out to be the beginning of several weekends that Jared and Aimee spent together during the winter and early spring of that year. They were happy and in love and their relationship grew in the days and weeks that followed. Jared was happier then he'd ever imagined he could be after his wife had left him. Aimee's prediction turned out to be correct. Jared was her Mr. Right. She fell head over heels in love with him. There was no doubt in her mind he was the man with whom she wanted to spend the rest of her life.

Jared asked Aimee to marry him in the summer. "Sweetheart, I love you more than I thought I could love anyone again. I want to be with you, not just on weekends but every day and night."

Aimee was surprised. She expected they'd get married, but not until she was out of school in two years. She had envisioned a huge wedding that would take months to plan. "I love you so, you know I do. I'm just not sure I want to get married this summer." Aimee didn't know what to say. She was afraid she'd lose him if she said no. "I need to think about this. I'm going home next weekend. Can I have some time to sort this out? Everything's happened so fast. I'll call you and we'll make plans for you to come to Fort Akers and meet my family. Okay? I'll let you know for sure then."

Watching Aimee drive off that afternoon, Jared's heart was heavy. He sensed she was having doubts about their relationship. "Damn it. Why did I do this? She's so young yet and she wants to finish college. She's not ready to get married. I need to give her some space."

Aimee's mind was churning during the drive back to IU. "Why did I do that?" she asked herself. "I love Jared!" There wasn't any doubt in her mind. "I'll marry him this summer if that's what he wants." Excitement filled her heart at the thought of being Mrs. Jared Bradley! "No one could ever compare to Jared. He's so gentle and loving and sweet." The more she thought about it the more she came to the realization that getting married was exactly what she wanted too. "I can't wait to tell Kendra and Mom and Dad about Jared."

On Tuesday morning, Aimee loaded up her car in order to head back home to Alfaland for the summer. She hadn't heard from Jared so she was determined that she would stop and see him and give him her answer. Yes, she would marry him this summer. She phoned before leaving Bloomington, but there was no answer. When she stopped by his apartment, he wasn't there. Aimee had to leave. She still had a three-hour drive ahead of her. "I guess I'll just have to call him once I get home to Alfaland."

Aimee felt she was a different person going home this summer. She'd left as child and now she felt like a woman, but she wished she had told Jared yes right away. There was not a doubt in her mind about how she felt. Just this short time she'd been away for him made her realize that.

Meanwhile, Jared had decided not to push Aimee, but would wait for her to call. He realized she had some things to sort out in her mind. He was sure he'd hear from her by the following Sunday. She would have been home by then, but she never phoned. A week passed. Nothing. His heart was broken, again. He just couldn't believe Aimee hadn't called. "Maybe she got home and decided she didn't want to be involved, but didn't have the heart to tell me," he told himself.

A month passed. He realized he'd lost her. Aimee probably decided, after being apart, that it was only infatuation, that she wasn't really in love after all. He'd scared her off by talking marriage. He'd lost two loves in one year. He felt like such a failure.

He began to have doubts about his own feelings after the second month had passed. "Maybe I had just been on the rebound. I had just lost Jessica. Maybe I was just fooling myself."

By the end of August, he knew Aimee would be back in school and going on with her life. Jared knew he also had to go on. He attempted to date, but he was lonely again.

He wondered what was wrong, why he always failed to make love work for him. He had so much love to give. Someday, somewhere in his future, he hoped someone would come along again, and the next time he would not lose her.

He sat in his office, taking one last look at the only pictures that he had of their time together. The pain was unbearable; He took the pictures and placed them at the back of his file drawer. It was time to go on, but he would never forget his special, little one, and the good times they'd had.

***

Setting at the side of her younger sister's bed, Kendra's mind pondered the dreadful heartbreaking words that the evil old man had spoken. She kept coming back to the same dead ends. What was Jared's relationship with Aimee? What secrets did Aimee hold inside her silent motionless body? Why hadn't Jared, in all their years of marriage, ever told her? There were so many unanswered questions and the sad conclusion, Kendra realized, was that she might never know the answers. She closed her eyes and shook her head. If only Jared hadn't been shot." She sighed. The anger swelled again inside her as she thought to herself. "I wish things could have been different," she said to Aimee. Realizing the irony of her thought, she rolled her eyes toward the ceiling. "In what way," she sighed, "I don't know."

"Oh Jared," she thought silently again. "I miss your body next to mine and the touch of your hands." She stared at Aimee Sue for a moment, unable to control her thoughts. "I wonder if you do, too. She stood. Kendra pushed the thought from her mind and left the room, returning only a few times over the next several months.

Chapter Eighteen

"Dad, if it hadn't been for Ian, Aimee Leigh, Jared Jr. and, Alfaland, I don't think I'd have made it through the last winter and the holidays. It was a cold, lonely winter."

"I know, sweetheart." Byron finished securing the pool cover they had just stretched across the pool. "You've had so much to deal with already in life." He put his arm around her shoulder. "And you've become a strong person. I'm proud of you."

"Thanks for all your help, Dad, I sure don't feel very young." Kendra wrapped her arm around her father's waist. "This summer's been a little better. It's been good for the kids to be outside, and me, too. I've spent most of my afternoons out here with the kids at the pool." Kendra looked at her father. "Did I tell you we managed to get CJ, our new colt, broke this summer? Ian spends hours riding. He so loves the farm. Sometimes we've doubled up and taken Aimee Leigh and Jared riding with us."

Kendra didn't mention it to her father, but Ian was more consolation to her than anyone else in the months following Jared's death. Kendra recalled how Jared had asked Ian to take care of his mother for him that night as he lay dying on the wet grass. She was aware that Ian considered Kendra his mother and, likewise, she regarded him as her son.

Arm-in-arm, Kendra and Byron strolled toward the wooden porch swing that was secured between two maple trees to the south of the swimming pool. "So, when are you and Jane leaving for the holy land?" Kendra asked.

They sat down and began to swing back and forth. "Next Wednesday. We'll be gone for four weeks." He looked at Kendra. "Are you sure you'll be all right?"

"Yes, Dad." She nodded. "We will be just fine."

Aimee Leigh came running out the back door carrying a small white baby kitten. Her pigtails were in disarray, with only one having the original red ribbon tied around it. Buster followed close behind in an effort to check out the kitten.

Aimee Leigh ran up to where they were swinging. "Will we be able to go camping this weekend, Grandpa?"

Byron lifted her up on his lap. "I'm afraid not, dumpling. I think your mommy and Jane are going to run you into town to look for school clothes Saturday afternoon." He looked back at Kendra. "Is Jared Jr. excited about starting kindergarten this year?"

The door slammed, and Jared and Ian came running out of the house.

"Ask him yourself," Kendra said with a grin. Kendra recognized, now that Jared Jr. was getting older, how he looked even more like Ian. "Same father, different mothers," she thought. She realized she was going to have to tell the family the truth, but she just couldn't bring herself to talk about it. Not yet.

"Grandpa, I'm starting school next week. See my new cowboy boots Mommy got me." He lifted his foot and pointed. "And I got a new school box and crayons and a backpack."

"I guess I don't have to ask, do I?" He looked at Kendra and laughed.

The next couple of months were hectic. Kendra was working

almost full time and the kids were busy with school activities. The cooler weather had moved in and the trees were losing their leaves. Kendra felt good to be active in the adult world again. She was getting along better everyday and again beginning to adjust to the changes in her life.

During mid-October, on a Saturday night, they had all retired early after an exhausting day of raking and burning leaves. Kendra had made a party of sorts out of it by purchasing hot dogs and marshmallows as an incentive to keep everyone's enthusiasm alive. It had worked.

Before drifting off to sleep, Kendra thought, "It's hard to believe Jared's been gone for a year." Always she would have this battle in her mind between missing him so and wondering what the truth really was. She wrestled most every night with the same thoughts. Later that night, something awoke Kendra out of a deep sleep. She was positive that she had heard someone. She lay quiet and listened. It must have been one of the kids. She glanced over at the clock. It was 2 a.m. Kendra lay in the darkness listening to see if she could hear it again.

In the bedroom upstairs, Aimee Sue slowly opened her eyes. It was dark in the room except for a dim light left on in the hallway that was cast through the frame of her door. She blinked her eyes several times. Aimee couldn't put her finger on it, but her room looked different somehow. She thought, "It's probably because I've been away to school the last couple of years." She glanced over at the windows. She hadn't noticed the new café curtains before. "Doesn't look like mom's style," she thought. "I didn't even notice them. I can't believe I didn't notice them before." She glanced at the night stand. It didn't look like her night stand. "Where did that picture of the little boy come from?" She noticed what looked like a child's school picture in a dark walnut wooden frame. He appeared to be maybe seven or eight years old. "I know that wasn't on my night stand when I went to bed." She tried to remember. She couldn't remember going to bed. "This is so weird. He doesn't look like anybody I know. Am I at home or am I somewhere else?" Her mind was blank.

Aimee began to move then came to the startling realization that she was terribly weak. It took extreme effort just to move her arm.

"What? Why am I hooked up to this thing?" Aimee asked when she noticed a tube taped to her arm. "Am I dreaming? What is going on?"

She tried to shout but was so weak. "Mom!" She panicked! Not getting any response, she tried to shout louder. "Mom! Dad!" she finally yelled into the silence. She was frightened and confused.

The adjoining door to her room swung open and, to Aimee's amazement, a strange older lady walked into her bedroom wearing a nightgown.

"Who are you?" Aimee asked! "What's going on here?"

A moment later a second lady, appearing to be of similar age as the first, entered the room.

"Am I dreaming? Who are you?" Aimee again asked.

"Aimee, don't be afraid," Sarah, in a calming gesture, lifted her hands toward Aimee. "We are your nurses that have been here to take care of you." Sarah glanced at Judy and then back to Aimee. She clasped her hands together. "My name is Sarah." She pointed to Judy. "And this is my sister, Judy."

"Take care of me?" Aimee asked, "I don't understand. Why? I'm not sick."

"Yes," Judy said, endeavoring to remain calm. "You've been…asleep."

"Asleep? That doesn't make any sense." She glanced at Judy and then to Sarah. "What do you mean?" Aimee asked in puzzlement. "I don't understand. "Where are my mom and dad?"

Kendra listened in silence. There it was again. One of the kids was calling for her. Which one was it? Aimee Leigh was in bed with her, so it couldn't be her. Kendra crawled out of bed and slipped on her robe and house slippers. She then headed toward Jared's room only to find him curled up along with Buster sound asleep. When the dog saw her, he jumped down off the bed and followed her. "It must be Ian," she thought. A moment of uneasiness seized her. "Ian, what is wrong?"

Kendra headed up the stairs and was startled when she discovered Ian standing on the landing. "Ian, honey, what's the matter?" She kneeled down in front of him and held him in her arms. "Are you all right?"

He responded, wrapping his arms around her neck. "She's awake," he whispered. "I heard her talking to Sarah and Judy." He was trembling.

Kendra didn't immediately grasp what he had said. She kissed him on the cheek. "Everything will be all right," she said.

Kendra then heard voices coming from Aimee's room. She and Ian's eyes locked for a moment in a mutual conclusion. Kendra turned and rushed into the room, Ian and Buster clinging close behind. Sarah, her short thinning gray hair in complete disarray, was standing on the left side of Aimee's bed, and Judy, barefooted, was on the right.

Incapable of believing her eyes, Kendra paused for a moment. There she was. Aimee lie awake in her bed. Flooded with shock, joy, and amazement, Kendra walked toward her little sister with tears streaming down her face. As the many years had passed, she'd just about given up on this miracle ever happening.

"Kendra, what's wrong? What's going on?" Aimee's voice quivered. "Why are you here? Is Aaron here too?"

She turned to Sarah who was now at the foot of the bed. "Go call Daddy."

Sarah nodded in agreement and turned to leave the room.

"And Doctor Scott," Kendra added. "Ask them to come right away. Thank God, Dad and Jane are back home. "And, call Lori, too." Sarah continued out the door.

"Daddy?" Aimee asked? "Where is he? Why isn't he home? It's the middle of the night, isn't it? Who is Lori? Why are you calling the doctor? Aimee's eyes fell upon Ian. "Who is the little boy?"

Kendra turned and became aware of Ian, with his arm locked around Buster's neck, standing half-beside and half-behind her, staring at Aimee.

"You're the little boy in the picture, aren't you?" Aimee glanced over at the picture on the night stand and then back to Ian. Her attention then turned back to Kendra. "Kendra, what's going on?" she pleaded. "I'm confused. That is Buster, isn't it? How did he get so fat? And, you look older."

"Yes, it is Buster," Kendra nodded her head, and then wiped her hand over her mouth while trying to gather her thoughts. "Ian," she said, "why don't you take Buster and go downstairs and wait for Grandpa?"

Aimee moved her eyes back and forth in deep thought, "Grandpa? Grandpa? Have I lost my mind? Kendra, is that your son? Ian, that's the name I wanted." Her voice dwindled to a whisper, shaking her head in disbelief, she looked at Ian and then to Kendra and said, "yesterday."

Ian willingly turned and left the room and Buster followed.

"Aimee," Kendra said, "what's the last thing you remember?"

Aimee looked down at a blue patch in her quilt and thought for a moment and then looked back at Kendra. "You and Aaron coming for dinner. For a cook-out down by the pond."

"What happened? Do you remember, Aimee?" Kendra asked.

"I don't understand. You and I were talking in the kitchen." Aimee grew quiet and stared at Kendra for another moment. She began again as if the memories were unfolding in her mind. "We were discussing Jared and..." She blinked several times. "I recall the phone rang." Aimee looked at Kendra.

Kendra nodded. "It was Aunt Jane."

Aimee's mind struggled for the truth. She stopped and stared across the room. "The tornado..." She again turned to Kendra. "There was a tornado! Oh God. It was over the woods! I can remember running for the basement! You were at the door." She stared out the window into the darkness. "That's all I can remember. The tornado must have hit." She looked back at Kendra. "The house is apparently still standing. We're at home, aren't we?" In an effort to reassure herself, Aimee nodded her head. "Right, we're at Alfaland?"

Kendra sat down on the edge of the bed and took Aimee's hand in hers. "Yes, Aimee, we are at Alfaland." She fought back tears. She shook her head in agreement. "The tornado did hit and it did a tremendous amount of damage. "And, you were badly injured from it." Kendra looked at Judy, who was still at the foot of the bed, then back at Aimee. "They found you in the bottom of the pool, barely alive." Kendra stroked Aimee's forehead with her fingers, brushing back her bangs. "You were in the hospital for a long time, Aimee, and then we hired these two ladies to help take care of you. They've been feeding, bathing and exercising you and tending to all your needs."

Aimee shook her head. "You can't be serious. This can't be true." Aimee sighed. "How long have I been like this?"

Kendra hesitated. She knew this had to be devastating, "It's been over eight years."

"Eight years?" Aimee asked in disbelief. She shook her head, looking up at the ceiling. "That's impossible."

"The things your sister are telling you are true, Aimee." Judy endeavored to be of assistance. "You've been in a coma, honey." She walked around to the opposite side of Aimee's bed, "Aimee, I really need to take your blood pressure and check your heart."

"Go ahead," Aimee said.

"Where are Mom and Dad?" Aimee asked. "Why aren't they here?"

Kendra's heart sank. It was as if no years had passed. The hurt and the memories of that horrible day leaped back in her mind. Tears flowed down Kendra's cheeks as she took Aimee's hand, "Mom was killed that day in the tornado."

Sarah walked back in the room and stood by Kendra and put her arm around her shoulder. "Your folks are on the way," she said.

"Mom's dead?" Aimee asked. "This just can't be! It has to be a nightmare!" She began to cry. Then she realized and questioned Sarah's words. "She just said they were on their way?"

Judy went into the bathroom, retrieved a warm washcloth and then gently began to wipe Aimee's forehead and face.

"Aimee Sue!" Her father's strong voice was jubilant from the doorway. "My sweet, Aimee... This day is a miracle!" Byron came into the room and Jane stepped beside the door and stayed in the hallway. They had already discussed that she would stay out of the picture until Aimee was more prepared.

Kendra was relieved at her father's presence. She stepped back so he could move in beside the bed. "She knows about Mom and that it's been eight years," Kendra whispered quickly in his ear as he slipped past her.

Byron leaned over and took his youngest daughter in his arms, feeling a mixture of joy and sorrow.

"Aimee, this is not going to be easy, I know," he said, "but you can do it. Together, we can do it. You're going to have to be strong, honey." He stroked her forehead. "There have been a lot of things happening that will take some adjusting to."

Sorrow gripped Kendra's heart. "Oh, Dad, if you only knew," she thought.

"Mommy, what are you doing?" It was Aimee Leigh standing in the doorway clinging to her Sponge Bob pillow. "Grandpa, what are you doing here?" she asked. She wiped her sleepy eyes with her hand.

Kendra prayed that Jared Jr. wouldn't wake up." She didn't want Aimee to hear that name yet. She felt a desperate desire to get out of the room.

"These can't be yours and Aaron's?" Aimee asked, smiling for the first time and looking from Ian, who had also re-entered the room, and back to Aimee Leigh in astonishment.

Kendra introduced them. "This is Ian and this is Aimee Leigh."

For a moment, Aimee's mouth dropped. She smiled through glossy eyes. "You gave them the names I said I liked." Aimee was touched. "They are so perfectly beautiful." She looked over at Kendra. "All I remember is that you were pregnant and now…Aimee Sue shook her head in disbelief. "Where's Aaron? I bet Aaron is one proud daddy!"

Thinking the same thoughts, Kendra and her father glanced at each other.

"Aimee," there is so much more we need to discuss, but first I think you should let Dr. Scott have a look at you and see what he thinks. He's out in the other room waiting to see you." At that, Byron got up and went out to get Dr. Scott, and Kendra took Ian and Aimee Leigh and shuffled them out of the room.

"I'll be back as soon as the doctor gets finished," Kendra said.

Kendra put Aimee Leigh back to bed and, since it was still early, she persuaded Ian to get into her bed also for a couple more hours of sleep.

"Are you going to tell her?" he asked.

"I'm going to check with Dr. Scott first." She stroked his forehead. "Now don't worry. It will all be just fine, sweetheart. Okay? You get some sleep." She leaned over and kissed his forehead.

He grabbed her around the neck. "I love you," he said.

"Oh, sweetheart, I love you, too." She kissed his cheek.

Weary, Kendra walked out to the kitchen, poured herself a cup of coffee and then sat down at the table with her father and Jane. There was no more putting it off. Her day of reckoning had come. If Kendra hadn't loved Jared so, she could almost hate him for putting her in this position.

"Dad," she began, "There's much more to Jared's death than I've been able to admit to you before. I should have, but I just couldn't bring myself to talk about it."

Mr. Patton was puzzled, unclear as to why she would bring this up tonight.

Kendra sat staring at her coffee cup, uncertain on how and where to begin. She took her index finger and stroked the top of her cup. Her heart was breaking. She looked at her father. "Dad, Jared didn't just get shot by burglars as all the papers reported. Jared was being blackmailed."

"Blackmailed?" His forehead wrinkled. "What for?"

Kendra leaned back in her chair, crossed her arms and took a deep breath pushing herself to continue on. "The chief knew about it, but agreed to keep it quiet because there was no need to expose the information. He left it up to me if I wanted to tell anyone." Kendra felt her heart pounding. "Jared tried to do what was right, Dad. He stood up to the blackmailer. That's why he was shot." Kendra fought back a mammoth swelling in her throat. "He came here to see me that night." She cleared her throat. The memories of that entire evening made Kendra nauseated. It was difficult to speak.

At this point, Byron realized that this was no trivial matter. Her father, seeing her struggling, endeavored to strengthen her by leaning over and gripping Kendra's hand between his large hands. "Go on, sweetheart."

She looked at him. "Jared was Ian's father, too."

It took a second for Byron to grasp the truth of what she was saying. His eyes glistened with moisture. "You mean he and Aimee?"

Kendra nodded. She began to sob uncontrollably.

"Oh honey, I am so sorry," Jane knelt down on the floor beside her chair and took Kendra's other hand.

"How in the hell did this happen?" Her father was beginning to absorb the seriousness of the situation. "I wonder if Jared ever gave any thought as to what he was going to do if Aimee had come out of her coma?" Byron placed his elbows on the table and, lowering his head, he positioned the palms of his hands over his temples. "How could he do this? How do we explain this to Aimee? And to Ian?"

"Ian already knows," Kendra said. "Poor little thing was right in the middle of everything the night Jared was shot. I'm not sure how much he heard." She shook her head. "There were some pretty terrible things said by the blackmailer, but Ian was able to speak to Jared before he died, which I know meant a lot to Ian." She reached over and placed her hand around her father's wrist. "He at least knows his father now. Also, there were some pictures that the blackmailer brought." Kendra sat back placing her hands upon her knees. "They are of Jared and Aimee Sue." Kendra looked down at the floor and then to her father. "I let Ian have them. He has them hidden in the wall in his room."

Kendra was relieved. She wasn't carrying this heavy weight alone any longer. She wished now she'd have talked to her father before instead of just tucking it away in the back of her mind and ignoring it.

Byron shook his head. "That child is quite the little person. He is so special. How did he ever handle this?" He rubbed his chin. "I can't believe he never mentioned a thing."

"Dad, that night when he and Jared talked, before he died, it was like the world stood still just for them, and gave them that moment." Kendra tilted her head and looked at her father. "It is a moment I'll never forget. It touched my heart dearly. I believe it was meant to be. I think Ian felt that way too."

Byron shook his head in silence.

Jane reached up and embraced Kendra. "There are a few rare times in this life when we experience those 'time stand still' moments. It seems that all too often they are bitter-sweet."

"That's strange." Kendra smiled. "Aaron talked about wishing time could stand still when we were at Spring Mill a couple of days before he died."

"You know," her father said, "Jane and I both commented on how you never talked about the night Jared was shot. We just felt like it was probably too upsetting for you to talk about it. That's why we didn't ask." He shook his head. "We had no idea."

There was a soft knock at the door. It was Lori Bradley. She came as soon as Sarah had called her. She was uncertain of what to expect. Kendra was grateful to have Lori join them and filled her in on all that had happened during this night.

"I'm so sorry," Lori said. "I wish there was something I could do or say that would make things better." She looked at them all sitting around the table. "Jared was my son. I loved him. I don't understand why he did what he did. I think he just wanted it to work out so bad, that he just ignored the truth and the facts. I wish he'd have talked to me about it. Maybe I could have helped, but he didn't. Please don't take this wrong, but, for me there is some good out of all this. He left me a grandson. I have no one else."

They were all silent for a moment and then Byron said, "And, a pretty special grandson. We are all going to have to do all we can to help him through this."

"Thank you, Byron," Lori said. "I'll do anything I can to help Aimee, too. What that girl must be going through right now?"

They continued to discuss the situation, and Dr. Scott soon joined them. "This has sure been the strangest case I have ever dealt with," he said.

"That's not the half of it," Byron said.

"I think I know what you are talking about, Byron. Kendra had me take a blood test of Jared when he died. You folks are going to have a lot to deal with, but as far as her physical condition, I've instructed Sarah and Judy to start giving her liquids, and I'll be back in the morning to check on her. Then, we'll decide what foods to begin with. We're going to leave the feeding tube hooked up for now. In a day or so, we'll attempt to get her up and begin the process of bringing her back to normal. She checks out very well. Much of the credit for that has to go to the care she's been given. Those two women have done a terrific job with her. They can't be beat. I believe Aimee's recovery will be swift. I am going to consult with some experts in the morning and see what they recommend."

"What about telling her everything that has happened?" Byron asked. "She doesn't even know Jane and I are married."

Dr. Scott placed his hand on Byron's shoulder. "You are just going to have to tell her everything as soon as possible. I don't recommend keeping things from her. It will take considerable patience and understanding on all your parts." He looked at Kendra, and then to Lori. "To give her the time she needs to deal with everything. It probably won't be easy."

Kendra, nearly in panic, shook her head back and forth, "Dad, I can't tell Aimee about Jared. I'm sorry. I just can't do it."

"Kendra listen to me, and understand this." Byron placed his hands on her shoulders. "Neither you nor Aimee have done anything wrong here." He squeezed her shoulders. "Now you stay strong on that point and don't beat yourself up. You are going to have to be the strong one for now. Your sister is going to need you and all of us."

Kendra nodded in agreement, and she and her father embraced.

"We need to get up there," Byron said. "This isn't going to be easy, but we've got to talk to her."

"It seems to me you are the only one that can do it," Jane said.

"I will go with you, if you want." Lori said. "It may help, me being Jared's mother."

"I think you're right," Byron said.

They agreed they would tell her everything that had happened in her life and family over the last eight years, while she had been in her coma, and answer any questions that she may ask.

Byron and Lori sat by Aimee's bed and told her about her mother's death, Aaron's death and that Kendra had lost her baby. They tried to cover everything that had happened over the last eight years.

After they had told her, they were both flabbergasted by her reaction.

"I know why she took Ian," Aimee said. "Because, she lost her baby, so she took mine."

"No Aimee that is not the way it was," Byron tried to explain. "You are not being fair, Aimee."

"Don't defend her, Dad. You all treat her like some kind of a hero in this. She's deceived you all. I bet you, even if she'd have known; she'd have taken Jared for herself."

"Aimee, that not true," Lori said.

"I don't know how she could have done this to me." Aimee said to Lori. "I hate her. She took my son. She made him think she was his mother. She didn't even try. She wanted him and Jared. That's all she cared about. She seduced him. I know how she is."

"Aimee, that's not true." Lori tried again. "She tried to keep Ian as your son. It was just hard with you being in the coma. She took care of him for you."

"She seduced Ian too. She's trying to make herself look like a hero in all this but she's not. All she cares about is Kendra."

Kendra and Jane waited at the kitchen table nearly an hour and a half before Byron and Lori appeared back in the kitchen. It was evident by their expressions that the discussion had not gone well. "We are going to have to give Aimee some time," Mr. Patton said. "I'm so sorry, honey, she is not taking this the way I had hoped at all, but we have to realize that she apparently loved Jared very much and

she's had so much to face and absorb all at once."
"Kendra looked at her father. "What do you mean, Dad?"
"She's upset right now," he said. His smile was reserved.
"She's not blaming me is she?" Kendra asked.
"Yes, she is." He placed his hand on her shoulder. "Lori and I have said about as much as we can say. She just can't seem to see past the fact that you and Jared were married. She can't handle it or the fact that he's dead. She's just not able to comprehend it all clearly yet. We felt we had to keep her as calm as possible, so Lori and I decided we'd better let it, and her, rest for now. The tragic thing is, at this point, Kendra, you'd better stay out of her room. She claims she doesn't want to see you. I'm sure in time her mind will clear. She's just not thinking straight."
"Unfortunately," Lori said shaking her head. "I'm afraid she's also got it in her head that she wants to move away from Alfaland as quickly as possible." Lori sighed and glanced at Byron. "Your father and I, in an effort to calm Aimee down, agreed we'd work on the arrangements right away and Kendra…" Lori hesitated a moment. "She wants to take Ian with her."
Kendra's heart sunk.
The next day Kendra avoided Aimee's room while the others were going in and out. In some ways, she felt like an outcast or a criminal in her own home. Kendra wanted to see and love her sister and share in the joy of her recovery. "We've already lost so many years and now were losing more," Kendra thought.
Within a week the arrangements were complete for Aimee and Ian to move into Byron's condo in Fort Akers. Sarah and Judy were going to take turns helping with her during the day until she was fully recovered but would now return to their own home each night. Byron had also made arrangements for Aimee to begin counseling. It seemed like all the hurt that Aimee felt came out in the form of hatred toward Kendra.
Aimee Leigh, Jared Jr., and Kendra reluctantly helped Ian pack his things. "I can't believe this is happening," Kendra kept thinking.
While they helped him pack his belonging into several suitcases

and boxes, the memories of the past eight years and the wonderful times they'd shared brought a pain to Kendra's heart that was difficult to conceal from Ian.

"Mom, I mean, Aunt Kendra," Ian asked. "Can I keep this as my room in case I get to come back? He put his hand down and stroked his favorite red and navy plaid wool blanket that he had just placed in a box.

"This room will remain your room for as long as you wish," she said, "and, you are always welcome here, anytime. Alfaland will always be your home, too." Kendra smiled while embracing him from the back. She placed her head against his and held him. "Do you recall, Ian, when I told you we have a special bond? No one can take that from us. You know I love you." She kissed the top of his head.

"I don't want to go," he said. "I don't want to leave you. Can't I stay here?"

"Ian, you need to go, and give it a chance. Grandpa and Aunt Jane will be there." Kendra's heart was sick.

"But, I don't want to leave Alfaland and you guys. This is my home…and…and you are my mom," he said.

"I'm not you mom, but I can be your best friend if you like." Kendra smiled at him. "Now, perk up, and give it a try. Okay."

"Okay," he said.

The little family held each other one more time and said their good-byes in Ian's room before Byron came and helped Ian carry his things down the stairs. Kendra had agreed to stay out of sight until they were gone with Aimee.

Uncontrollable tears kept reappearing on Kendra's cheeks while she sat on the floor and watched Jared and Aimee Leigh playing with a Nerf basketball that was hanging on Ian's door. She wiped her eyes with the top of her hands and then wiped her hands on the side of her jeans. "Why am I paying such a price for just trying to be happy?" she asked herself. "I've waited so long for Aimee to wake up, and now it has turned into such a nightmare. Why does life always have to be so complicated and painful?" Kendra couldn't help but believe that her sister would get her head on straight soon and this would all be over.

"Are you all right, Mom?" Aimee stood in front of her mother holding the Nerf ball in her hands.

"Yeah, I'm fine, honey." Kendra smiled and patted Aimee's arm. She got up on her feet, grabbed the ball, and tossed it at the hoop, making a basket.

Kendra heard the vehicles drive away, and she and the two children made their way back down to the main floor of the big empty house, the house that they would now share alone.

They were shocked and surprised when they walked into the kitchen, and found Ian on the porch with all his bags and boxes surrounding him.

"Ian!" Kendra couldn't hide her relief. "What happened?"

"She changed her mind," he said. Ian also looked relieved.

Jared and Aimee flew to embrace Ian, whom they had grown to consider was their brother. Screaming and jumping up and down, the two were unable to contain their excitement. Together, the three of them grabbed all his belongings and began to return them back up to Ian's room on the third floor.

Two weeks later, while the four were having breakfast, Jared asked. "Mommy, can we go see Grandpa?"

"No, not yet, honey, maybe Grandpa will come to see us this weekend." Kendra pulled a cookie sheet of cinnamon toast from the oven and poured him some more hot chocolate.

"I don't see why Aimee Sue had to leave," Aimee Leigh said bouncing her toast up and down in her hot chocolate and dribbling it across the table to her mouth.

Kendra slid the cup under Aimee's chin. "I don't either, sweetheart."

Byron and Jane had kept Kendra posted on Aimee Sue's progress. Physically, she was almost recuperated, but her attitude toward Kendra had not wavered one bit. It was putting a strain on the entire family.

Kendra heard a car door slam outside, and Jane and her father came in the back door.

"We were just talking about you." Kendra hugged them both.

"The kids were saying they wanted to see you and here you are." The little ones ran to embrace them.

Byron was right to the point. "How would you like to have your nephew permanently?"

"Yes. Yes. "The two younger ones yelled in unison.

"We'd love him," Kendra smiled at Ian.

Byron went on to explain. "Aimee, it is apparent, is just not able to cope with having a child and it is obvious that it won't work for either one of them." Byron continued. "Unfortunately Aimee's mental state is not improving very much."

"It appears as if she is going to take some time healing," Jane said. "Kendra, she hasn't changed in her attitude toward you but to our surprise and relief she's agreed to turn the guardianship of Ian over to you. She says she just can't think of him as her son."

"We believe she's realized that this would be the best for Ian," Byron concluded.

As the days continued, there was a lifting of spirits at Alfaland now that Ian was home to stay.

During the next few months, Kendra began to find that the new freedom, and less responsibility, in the house wasn't so bad after all. The only things she had to concern herself with were the children. Kendra did some wallpapering and redecorating on the second floor and moved Aimee Leigh and Jared Jr. to their own rooms, which they loved.

Kendra felt there was hope. She was going to make it. She only wished that this conflict with Aimee would end and that her family could be united again.

Chapter Nineteen

"Will you please hold still, wiggles?" Kendra attempted to secure the blue plastic floaters around Aimee's tiny arms.

"Hurry." Aimee bounced up and down. "Annie and I are going back in the water," she said after stuffing what was left of an ice cream sandwich into her petite little mouth and then wiping the remainder off her hands and face with her beach towel. Aimee Leigh was having too much fun to waste her day standing still for any length of time. She tossed the towel back down on the blanket beside Kendra, grabbed Annie's hand, and they ran full speed down the beach and splashed into the salty water.

Seventeen-year-old Anna Yoder was Aimee Sue and Jared Jr.'s baby sitter who had been elated when Kendra invited her to join them on their Christmas vacation in Florida to help with the children. Annie, as she wished to be called, was a somewhat quiet person but was dependable and trustworthy with the children. She had never been outside of Indiana before.

For two hours, Jared and Ian had been working to build a giant sand castle. Kendra didn't have the heart to tell them that the tide was going to wipe it out in the next few hours. Observing the two boys, Kendra noted how, except for their height, they looked like twins with their light blond curly hair and beautiful blue eyes. A reminiscent smile came over her face as she thought, "They look like two little miniature Jareds playing there together."

Kendra couldn't help but wonder how things would be right now if Jared were still alive. "No matter how deceiving he was," she thought, "or how much pain he brought to me and my family, I just cannot hold any hatred in my heart toward him. I can't imagine, though, how difficult this all would have been with Aimee if he were still alive." She had to admit, sick as it is to say, "It was probably for the best."

Sighing, Kendra lay back on the lounge chair and pulled her wire-rim sunglasses back down over her eyes. This vacation was bringing about a tremendous healing for all of them, but especially for her. She loved the endless white sandy beaches, the gentle, repetitious sound of the ocean slapping against the shore, the sea gulls soaring overhead, and the warm sunshine. It was uplifting and refreshing and the weather pattern this winter had been one of the warmest on record for Florida.

Arrangements had been made with her grandparents to use their luxurious condominium at Long Boat Key on the gulf coast of Florida during the Christmas holiday. Kendra had made the decision that this would be one way to avoid the uncomfortable situation in Indiana with Aimee Sue over the holidays.

Kendra regretted the fact that the children were going to miss Christmas with the rest of the family, but they didn't appear to be suffering. Besides, Kendra had to admit, she felt more relaxed and at peace then she had in a long time. "We'll have many years in the future to spend at Alfaland," Kendra thought. "It's just so good to get away from everything for a while."

Byron had agreed to keep in touch with Tony, her manager at the *Gazette*, and inform her if there were any problems, and George was taking good care, as usual, of the animals and the farm.

On the third evening after they had arrived, while sitting at the dinette eating a pizza, Jared Jr. picked up the TV remote and began flipping through the TV channels looking for something to watch.

"Stop, hold it," Kendra said as he flipped past a local news broadcast. "Flip it back. Please, sweetheart?"

Jared pushed the buttons and switched it back to the news channel. It was a news broadcast taking place from the lobby of a prestigious hotel on Tampa Bay where the local disc jockey was conducting an interview with Joey Dubious.

Kendra listened to every word of the interview. "Wow, Joey looks terrific," she thought, "only maybe a bit older. Let's see, he would be thirty-eight now." Kendra's heart soared with excitement. Cherished memories that were dormant for many years flooded back to life.

Joey was going to be giving two performances in the Tampa Bay area on the following Saturday night. Kendra grabbed a pen from her purse and jotted down the phone number they gave for ordering tickets.

"Mom, have you lost your mind or what?" Jared asked. "What do you care about this for? Can I change it now?"

"Do you know this guy or something?" Ian asked.

"I sure do, honey! Joey used to work for the *Gazette* before he became famous. I haven't spoken to him in many, many years."

"You mean that guy is from Fort Akers? Wow, I didn't know that. He's been on TV before. He's really famous."

"He's cool," Annie said. "He's good, too. I like his music. You mean he actually lived in Fort Akers? Is that what Dubois Plaza got its name from?"

"It sure is," Kendra said.

"Why don't you call him, Mom?" Aimee asked. She pounced on her mother's lap and wrapped her small arms around Kendra's neck.

"I believe I will, sweetheart. Hopefully he'll still remember me," Kendra said, feeling some doubts. "I'm sure he will. We were close friends at one time. Joey has a fantastic voice and he's written several hit songs. Do you remember 'When Love Dies'? You've heard me play that CD, I'm sure."

"Is he the one that sings that? I didn't know you knew him, Mom!" Ian said with excitement. "You play that a lot!"

"I didn't know you knew him either, Mrs. Bradley," Annie said.

"Can we meet him Mommy?" Jared asked.

"We'll see, honey." She raised her eyebrows. "Maybe."

After returning from a peaceful stroll along the beach, Kendra found the telephone number for the hotel where Joey was staying. With apprehension, she took a deep breath and dialed the number. "A lot has changed," she thought, "Joey may not even care to associate with a common country girl from the past."

Oh course, she hadn't thought about the fact that the front desk would be suspicious. Kendra hadn't considered fans. "You say your name is what?" The voice at the other end seemed to be humoring her. "Sure, okay, you're an old friend of Mr. Dubious. I'll be sure to tell him." She left her name and the telephone number at the condo and her cell number.

Kendra stayed up with Annie until twelve-thirty watching a movie on TV and then went to bed. At one-thirty, Annie was shaking her. "Mrs. Bradley, you have a phone call."

Kendra took a moment to collect her bearings, then slipped on her robe and hurried out into the living room to answer the phone. "I hope there isn't anything wrong back home," she thought.

"Hello, this is Kendra," she said.

"Kendra, how are you?"

"Joey?" Kendra rubbed her eyes. "Joey, is that you?" A smile appeared on her sleepy face.

"Yeah," he said, "I was out practicing for Saturday night's show. We just got in and I had this message that you had called. I couldn't believe it. It's so great to hear from you. Where are you?"

"I wasn't sure I was going to be able to get through to you. It's great to hear your voice, too." Kendra told Joey where they were residing and that they were planning on staying through the holidays. "We were hoping to get tickets for your show Saturday night."

"How many do you need? I'll get them for you."

"Well, I'm sure there's no way my babysitter would want to miss

ALFALAND

this, so in order for her to go I have to take everybody."

"How many do you have now?"

"Three. Two." Kendra stammered, feeling a bit foolish, "Well, actually, I have three."

"You don't know?" Joey laughed.

Kendra laughed with him. "It's a long story. I actually have two of my own, and my sister's son, who is like my own. Do you remember Aimee Sue was in a coma and pregnant when you moved away? This is her son."

"I certainly do remember. I spent a lovely Thanksgiving with you and your family in her bedroom at Alfaland several years ago."

"That's right." Kendra recalled. "That was a beautiful Thanksgiving, wasn't it? I remember how it snowed."

"So how are things at Alfaland? I've always loved that place."

"Just as beautiful as ever; the kids and I are living there now."

"Your dad's not living there?" he asked.

"No, he and Jane moved to a condo in Fort Akers. They like to travel a lot."

"I think about that place often." Joey smiled. "Did you ever find the father of Aimee's baby?"

She hesitated. "Yes we did," she said. "It's really complicated. Maybe sometime I'll explain it to you."

"So how is Jared?" Joey noticed she hadn't mentioned him. "Jared. Isn't that his name?"

Silence fell over their conversation. Kendra groped for words.

"Kendra, are you there?"

"Apparently, you didn't hear," she said.

"Hear what?" he asked.

"Jared had become a police officer for the Fort Akers police department and he was shot a little over a year ago."

"Shot? Kendra I don't believe it. I'm so sorry. I didn't know. I've sort of lost touch," he said. "So you have to live through that hell a second time." The tenderness that Joey had always shown her was still present in his voice. "How are you doing?"

"Okay." Kendra wanted to change the subject. "So tell me, what has your life been like, being a famous star like you are?"

"There are a lot of complications that go along with fame and fortune." There was sadness to his voice. "I'm sort of running out of gas, if you know what I mean. It's been fun but not as much fun as you would think. It's all too fast paced for me. I wouldn't want to go on like this forever."

"I can see what you are saying," Kendra said.

The two old friends continued their conversation for over two hours. "A lot of water's passed under the bridge." Joey sighed. "I've been in and out of many relationships but nothing's ever seemed to stick."

Kendra recalled, just that day, seeing him on the cover of a well-known magazine with one of the most famous models in the world.

"Could we come over and see you tomorrow afternoon?" Joey asked.

"I'd love that. So would the kids! They can't believe I really do know you....you said we?" She asked. Kendra hoped he didn't mean he was bringing a lady friend.

"I take my bodyguards with me everywhere. They are like family. My life is strange, Kendra." He didn't tell her how lonely his life had become. Hearing her voice again was like water in the desert.

It took Kendra another hour before she could get back to sleep after hanging up the phone. Her mind churned over the memories of Joey and those carefree days when she and Aaron and Joey were friends. The days when the future was enticing and responsibilities few, and then later, when it was just her and Joey.

Hearing Joey's voice again was like a healing medicine to her, just as it had been many years before. Kendra grew more and more excited at the prospect of seeing Joey tomorrow.

Chapter Twenty

Back at Fort Akers Byron, Jane and Aimee Sue were just finishing up breakfast.

"How are you doing this morning Aimee?" Byron asked.

Aimee looked at him, "Dad, physically, I'm doing pretty well. Getting out and walking, like you suggested has helped. But, I can't seem to shake this sadness that I feel. I feel like I'm in a different world they everybody else. I don't seem to fit anywhere. I don't understand. It just seems like Kendra has everything and I have nothing. I had a son and I don't even know him. He's a stranger to me. You two have each other and a good life." Tears came to her eyes. "Where do I fit?"

"Aimee, we've had eight years to adjust to all that you are going through in a few weeks." Byron said. "There were rough times for us, too. We went through all that pain and sadness that you are suffering. Kendra had a lot of ups and downs after losing Aaron and the baby. She, too, felt as if her world had ended."

"I was so happy with Jared, Dad. I can't believe he's gone. We were going to get married. Why do you think he married Kendra? I can't accept it. I can't believe it, yet I know it's true. You've all told me."

"Sweetheart, you've got your whole life ahead of you."

"I lost a bunch of my life," Aimee said. She wiped her eyes. "I've lost the best years. How do I begin?"

Jane gave her a tissue.

"Honey, you've got to get over this hatred of Kendra. She is not the problem. The problem is you've lost the man you loved, your mother, and eight years of your life."

"But she lived with the man I love. She had children with him." Aimee said. "I get ill just thinking about it. I can't stand being near her."

"Do we still want to go looking for a car for you today?" Byron asked. "Let's get ready and go. It will be good for you to get out for awhile."

Aimee thought for a moment. "Okay, we'll go. I don't know why, but I'll go."

"Aimee, it will get better," Byron assured her. "You'll get through this. Give yourself some time. Trust in God, and pray about it."

"We'll help you," Jane said.

In Florida, Kendra sat at her grandmother's antique dressing table in front of an oval-shaped mirror, endeavoring to style her hair. She was anxious about her appearance. After several minutes, and a variety of attempts, she came to the conclusion to leave the back hanging down and pull the sides up and secure them with a floral scarf on the top of her head. She hadn't been this concerned about her appearance in months. She crossed her legs, folded her arms across her lap and stared at herself in the mirror. "I wonder," she asked herself, "If I'll appear old to Joey? After all, he's been with the most beautiful women in the world." Kendra smiled and shook her head. "It's hopeless." Placing her hand under her chin and her elbow on her knee she asked herself, "I wonder if he's had a relationship with any of them?" She rolled her eyes and laughed. "I'm losing it. Get a hold of yourself, girl," she said out loud to the image in the mirror. Nearly ten years had passed since she'd last seen Joey. "Ten years," she said. Kendra leaned with her nose only inches from the mirror. "My eyes look a little older, but the body's not too bad for thirty-two."

She stood up, turned sideways and laid her hands on her flat stomach. "Considering the lack of attention," she told herself, "not too bad. I am going to start taking better care of myself." Kendra again turned her slim body from one side to the other before the mirror. The red shorts and halter top she'd purchased earlier that morning with the floral scarf tied in her hair gave her just the boost she needed.

She took one more final inspection, then sprayed on a bit of perfume before leaving the bedroom and strolling out onto the beach to join the family. "Maybe he won't even show up," She thought.

Ironically, shortly after reclining in her lawn chair, Joey's newest hit, "Sweet Sweet Something" began to play over the radio. The Tampa Bay radio station had been playing his music in an effort to promote the Saturday night performances.

After a quick check to make sure all the kids were accounted for, she laid her head back on the chair, closed her eyes and made an effort to relax.

Moments later, she felt warm hands gently pressed over her closed eyes. Assuming it to be one of the children, she turned to discover Joey smiling down at her from behind the lawn chair. Jumping to her feet, she stretched out her arms and, for the first time in many years, the two old friends embraced.

"It's so good to see you, Kendra." Joey wrapped his long arms around her shoulders. He stepped back and smiled the charming little grin Kendra had always adored. "It's been a lot of years," he said, shaking his head.

"Too many," Kendra nodded and smiled back. "Joey, you look fantastic!" She stood back and looked him over. "You look like a star." He still had the same light sandy brown mustache. His slightly curly hair was not long, but did stick out about two inches from under his hat in the back. "You are more handsome than I had remembered." She didn't mention it, but did notice his eyes appeared a little tired.

Joey looked again into the treasured face of the only woman he had ever really loved. "Oh god, it's great to see you." he said, blinking back a hint of tears and embracing her body for the third time. "The years have been good to you," he said. "Never would I have believed that you could look any better." He shook his head. "But you are more beautiful than ever." Joey couldn't keep his eyes off of her. Something he hadn't felt in many years had ignited inside of him.

He became aware of several little eyes behind Kendra staring at him. "These must be yours," Joey smiled and eyed the dripping wet, sunburned faces standing in a line-up behind Kendra.

Kendra couldn't help but chuckle at the expressions on the faces of her family. Aimee's chin had dropped and her eyes stared in amazement at Joey. Kendra introduced each of them to Joey, including Annie, who was taken aback by the encounter.

Joey then introduced the gentlemen standing to each side of him. "Danny McCormick and Elvis Elliott," he said, pointing to them. "These are my two top body guards. I call them my shadows."

Danny was ruddy-looking and appeared to be in his fifties. Elvis was young and handsome, no more than twenty-five.

"It looks fairly secluded and quiet around here, do you mind if we join you? Joey asked.

"We'd love it." Kendra smiled.

The afternoon was one of continual conversation between Joey and Kendra. They transferred back and forth between the beach and the patio, sipping several margaritas as Danny kept refilling their glasses for them. They discussed the directions that both their lives had taken over the years. Kendra explained the entire situation concerning Jared and his death, Ian, and also Aimee's rejection of her.

"It's hard to comprehend what Jared did to you," he said. "He's the father of both." He paused and shook his head. "It's almost sick."

"I know," Kendra said. "I haven't been able to figure it out. I've actually given up on ever knowing why." She looked at Joey, "I can go on but I don't know about Aimee."

"Has anyone tried talking to her?" Joey asked.

"Dad and Aunt Jane, and even Jared's mother have, but to no avail. I've wanted to but they all think I should stay away because I would upset her more. She is just so confused. It's hard to comprehend how it must feel to lose eight years out of your life. I've decided I'm not going to let it get me down and go on with my life. I feel so very sorry for her though. I have my children and a life. She has nothing."

"It is hard to realize," Joey said.

"She is going to counseling. Hopefully, they'll be able to help her soon. It's painful to see her. Well I guess I don't see her, in this state."

"I can understand," Joey said.

Joey shared his life and experiences over the last ten years. "I realize I've been more fortunate than I had ever dreamed I would be. I just miss being normal sometimes. When you're living the fast life and in the celebrity world, sometimes it's easy to lose yourself and your identity. I sometimes have to regroup and take control again, you know what I mean? Danny's been a tremendous help. He's more than an employee. He's a friend. I don't know what I'd do without him." He smiled at Danny.

"You'd fall flat on your face," Danny said as he slid the patio screen open with his foot and brought them another drink. He sat down at the patio table with them and lit up a cigarette. "So, you are Kendra Patton," he said. "I feel as if I know you. I've heard Joey speak of you so much. He said you were good looking, and that's a fact."

Kendra blushed. "Joey talked about me?" she asked.

Danny nodded, "Often, quite often. Tell me, how did you ever stay out of the limelight yourself? You could have been a model."

Kendra laughed at his flattery. "No talent is my only drawback, Danny. Anyhow, I don't think Fort Akers could handle another famous celebrity, and besides, I already have a road named after me." She grinned. "Of course, Joey has an entire mini-mall named after him. Dubious Plaza." She poked Joey in the side with her toe.

"So how is Alfaland?" Joey asked. "I think of that place often. It's like a friend. I even wrote a song about it."

"That's such a perfect way to describe it Joey." She thought for a minute. "It is a friend. It's just as lovely as ever." She smiled. "Always peaceful, always beautiful."

"Let's go for a walk on the beach," Joey said. He grabbed her foot in his hand and squeezed it.

"Let's," Kendra agreed. She was enjoying his company again and feeling more than a little tipsy from all the drinks. Kendra wasn't accustomed to drinking, except for a few special occasions.

"Elvis and I'll help keep a watch over the little ones, you two go ahead," Danny said. "Do you have your radio, Joey?" he asked.

"Got it." Joey patted his pocket as he slipped the cotton terrycloth jacket on over his swimsuit and grabbed a pack of Winston's and his sunglasses off the table.

"So when did you start smoking, Joey?" Kendra asked.

"About two days after I hired Danny, actually. I've been going downhill ever since." He grinned and took a quick glance back at Danny.

The warmth of the Florida sunshine embraced them. They headed north down the endless sandy beach, strolling in and out of the water, letting it wash across their feet as it splashed up on the sand.

Kendra had slipped on a black shirt over her swimsuit. She was feeling a bit silly and more alive then she had in a long time. It was impossible to be down with the sunshine, the ocean, and Joey by her side. She felt like a teenager.

"What are you thinking about?" Joey asked, seeing her staring in deep thought out over the ocean.

"This is really strange, but a thought just flew through my mind. Something that Aaron had said the day before he was killed."

"What's that?" Joey reached over and took her hand.

"We were standing on a foot bridge at Spring Mill State Park and Aaron made the comment that it was so beautiful and peaceful." She looked at Joey. "He said he just wished he could make time stand still."

Joey put his arm around her shoulder, pulled her close to him, and kissed her hair above the ear. "I understand exactly what he meant." She was surprised but not displeased by his kiss. "So do I," Kendra said. She looked down and slid her big toe through the sand.

After they had walked more than half a mile, Kendra realized that there were several people walking near them. Soon many more appeared, and she then realized that they were staring at Joey, stretching their necks and whispering as they edged closer and closer to them. Kendra felt a little nervous. She noticed Joey put his radio up to his mouth and say something, just before people were swarming at them from every direction. Kendra got pushed aside as the crowd surrounded Joey. Several girls were touching him and pulling at his jacket. "This is scary." Kendra thought. She felt nauseated and hot.

Fear grabbed her heart when, out of the corner of her eye, she saw a man with a gun tucked inside his waistband rushing toward Joey in the crowd. "Oh God," she screamed, "Not Again!" She felt her knees buckle and everything went black before her.

Kendra, wake up. Kendra, are you all right? It's okay, please, Kendra?" Joey kept repeating her name.

Kendra opened her eyes and realized that she was lying on the beach with Joey kneeling over her. She grabbed Joey and cried as she held him. "Joey you're all right."

"I'm okay. I'm just fine," he said. He wiped the hair out of her face. "I'm afraid this happens quite often if I go out. I should have warned you; one of the pitfalls of the fame." He smiled as he knelt by her side, holding her in his arms.

"But, the gun?" she asked. "What about the man with the gun? Did you see him?"

He hugged her. "Kendra, I'm so sorry. That's Sherm, another one of my bodyguards that is always with me. That's why I called them when the crowd began getting out of control. I've been through this before."

"Joey, how do you live like this?" Kendra insisted. She sat up feeling more than a little foolish. To make matters worse, Kendra became aware that the crowd was still there, only larger, and they were staring at her. The only thing that was holding them back to an acceptable distance was the presence of several bodyguards and police officers. She noticed several people with cameras that were snapping photos of her.

Joey helped her up and brushed the sand out of her hair and off her jacket. They were then escorted back to her apartment in a police squad car.

By the time the officers had dropped them off, they were both laughing about the whole incident, including the officers.

"I feel like such a fool," Kendra said.

"You realize that you are going to probably be on the national news tonight?" Joey informed her while they walked up the walk and around the building to the patio.

"Not really, you are kidding." She looked over at him, uncertain whether to believe him or not. "Joey, tell me you are joking."

"I'm just as serious as I can be." He began to laugh.

"You didn't tell anyone my name did you?" she asked.

Joey gained control of himself. "No, I didn't and the guys wouldn't either. You're safe. You can bet the tabloids will be struggling frantically to find out who you are though. You were so beautiful stretched out there, stone cold, on the beach." He teased her. Joey threw his arms and head back and closed his eyes imitating her. "I want to make sure I get one of those pictures."

Kendra punched him in the stomach.

Later that evening, every newspaper and news broadcast in the country showed Joey Dubious, the famous country and western singer on the beach in Florida, with what they called an overly emotional female fan, passed out beside him.

Kendra felt like she could die. She prayed no one would ever know she was the one in the photo. Unfortunately, she discovered that her family back home saw it when her father called that night.

"Kendra," he said, "you appear to be having fun on the beach there in Florida."Are you okay?"

"Yes, I'm fine. Just a little too much to drink mixed with the heat.

Oh Dad, I'm sorry you saw that. I'm so embarrassed."

"I can imagine," he said, "but I was really thrilled to see you were with Joey. How is he?"

"He's great, Dad. We really had a wonderful afternoon. We are all going to his concert Saturday night and he's flying us all to Disney World on Thursday in his private jet. Would you believe?"

"I bet the kids will enjoy that," he said." He was quiet for a moment and then said, "I wanted to talk to you about Aimee. She seems to be really depressed the last few days. I don't know," he said, "she just is having such a rough time."

"I wish I could talk to her Dad," Kendra said. "I miss her so."

"You know Kendra, that's strange that you should say that," her father said, "because Jane and I have been talking and we think maybe you should try to talk to her. I don't think it could make things any worse. What do you think?"

"Oh Dad, I'd love to talk to her. I think that's a good idea," Kendra said. "As soon as I get home, I'll do that. I think it would be better to talk to her in person."

"I agree." I wish you were coming home sooner," he said.

Chapter Twenty-One

"Mom, the limo is here." Ian shouted from the front deck where he had been anxiously watching for the last hour. The camera Joey had given him was dangling from his neck.

Saturday night had arrived, and they had been given front row seats at Joey's sold-out concert. Annie was going to bring the children back after the first performance, but Kendra was staying for both performances.

"This doesn't make any sense," Kendra thought. "I don't understand why my stomach's all tied up in knots. It's Joey's concert, not mine." She applied the finishing touches of pink blush to her cheeks and with shaky fingers slipped the posts of her gold tassel earrings into her pierced ears. She was wearing a black floor length strapless gown which slid snuggly over her slender body.

"Are you coming, Mommy?" Aimee asked. She stuck her nose in the bedroom door. "You look so pretty, Mommy!"

"Thank you sweetheart," Kendra knelt, for a moment, in front of her daughter and straightened the gathered skirt she was wearing that had twisted sideways. She then placed her hands on Aimee's small shoulders and smiled. "You look pretty terrific yourself." Aimee was proudly wearing a white Mickey Mouse shirt and a brightly flowered floor length cotton skirt. Joey had purchased them for her at Disney World. Thursday he had flown them to Orlando, along with Elvis, Danny, several other body guards and some of their wives and children.

"I think I had as much fun as the kids," Joey had admitted on their flight back. They were totally exhausted by the time Joey's jet had landed them back in Sarasota late Thursday night.

Because of Joey, Kendra wondered if they would ever be able to come back down to earth after this was all over, herself included. They were being treated like royalty everywhere they went.

Kendra took Aimee's hand and followed her out to the limousine where the others were anxiously waiting. "This is getting to be a habit," she thought. She hadn't driven a car all week. They were escorted into the amphitheater amidst a noisy crowd of anxious fans.

"This atmosphere would be exciting even if we didn't know Joey," Annie shouted over the kid's heads to Kendra.

"Over here, folks," Danny was motioning for them. "I have you seated right here on the front row beside me. I have a little something for you that Joey wanted me to give you." Danny handed each one of them a t-shirt with Joey's picture on it like the ones they had seen being sold at the entrance.

"This is so thrilling. I'll never forget this, Mrs. Bradley," Annie said.

"It is, isn't it? Kendra said. So many things have been happening so fast since Joey came into the picture. The last four days have been a whirlwind."

Jared Jr. got up from his seat and walked over and stood in front of his mother. "Are we going to sing with Joey tonight?"

Kendra and Danny laughed. "No, not today, Jared, "Kendra stroked the hair on the side of his head."That was a practice session we went to on Tuesday. I don't believe we would want to sing in front of all these people."

"I want to be a singer like Joey when I grow up," Jared said.

"Anything is possible," Kendra smiled at him.

He hugged her and then walked back to his seat.

"Who'd have ever imagined this would happen to shy, gentle Joey Dubious?" Kendra said turning to look at Danny. "My mind keeps wondering back to the *Gazette* and the time Joey worked there. I hated to see him go."

"He hated leaving," Danny said.

"He did?" Kendra asked. "Why would you think that?"

"Believe me, I know that." Danny said. "He never would have left if he hadn't lost you."

Kendra stared blankly at him. She wasn't sure what he meant.

The lights dimmed and the spotlight zoomed toward the rear of the stage. The crowd screamed and applauded as Joey walked up the steps to the center of the stage and began to sing one of his most popular hits.

"He looks absolutely gorgeous," Kendra thought. She chuckled, "I'm probably only one of a thousand in the audience thinking the exact same thing. I'm so proud of Joey." A sight grin appeared over her face realizing that Joey was affecting her, just as much as he was all the other women in the audience. "There is just something about him," she thought as she watched him sing.

Joey looked striking, in slim fitting jeans, a white half buttoned shirt and black jacket along with his usual white cowboy hat and black boots. Kendra was pleased to see he was wearing the gold cross and chain necklace that she had sent him earlier in the day. She'd had engraved the words, *"Thanks—Kendra"* on the back of it.

Joey smiled at her and the kids several times during his performance.

Kendra leaned over and whispered to Danny. "This is going to be a night they'll all remember."

"Before I go on," Joey said, "I want to take a minute and have a group that is very, very special to me from my home town, Fort Akers, Indiana, to stand. They've made my visit here in Florida the greatest week I've ever had. His voice became softer. "They are like family to me." He smiled at them and motioned for them to stand. "I hope I've helped make their visit here a special one, also." The kids, overwhelmed, nodded before they sat back down in their seats. Aimee Leigh slapped her hands over her face and giggled. Ian and Jared Jr. both waved at Joey.

During the break between performances Kendra, Danny, and Elvis helped get the children back to the limousine with Annie and then found their way backstage to Joey's dressing room.

Kendra and Elvis walked into the dressing room and Joey signaled with his hand for Elvis to shoo everyone else out, which he did. Before Elvis left, he gave Kendra an affectionate kiss on the cheek and, without a word, left the room.

Staring at the handsome celebrity-friend that stood before her Kendra thought, "In some crazy way, I feel like a queen before a king."

They slipped into each other's arms, each holding the other as if they may somehow lose the other if they were to let go.

"I have so many regrets," Joey said while embracing her. "How was I tonight?"

"Joey you were fantastic. That was a strange experience hearing all those women screaming after you. I was proud of you." She leaned her head back and looked into his eyes, "And to know you. Your voice was, as always, unique." She continued to look into his brown eyes. "You are unique, Joey."

Joey stepped back, touching her soft tanned face with his fingertips. "Kendra, seeing you has brought to life in me something that had died years ago. You mean more to me than fame or all the riches in the world. I've always loved you and only you. My life's never been complete since you walked out of it."

"Joey, why didn't you tell me how you felt? I thought my feelings were all one-sided, and besides, I didn't want to mess up your life. I thought you and Julie had gotten back together."

"I was such a fool," Joey said. "I felt so guilty when I realized I had fallen in love with you, my best friend's wife. I felt like it would be showing disloyalty towards Aaron if I said anything. It all sounds so ridiculous now."

"Sweet, Joey," Kendra said. "How could I have been so blind and foolish?" She stroked the side of his face. "I loved you back then, I just wouldn't admit it to myself, and I love you now."

There was a light tapping on the door. "It's me Danny." He peeked in the door. "You need to get ready, Joey, it's about time. Sorry." He grinned. "Your fans are calling you."

"Okay, give us just a minute," Joey said. Danny closed the door.

Oblivious to the voices, reporters, and fans outside the door, they kissed one more time. Joey whispered in her ear. "In a way time has finally stood still for us."

Kendra returned to her same seat in the audience.

After Joey had sung several songs, Danny leaned over and spoke in Kendra's ear. "I never tire of listening to him. If it's possible, he's doing even better in the second concert."

"The audience seems almost spellbound," Kendra whispered back as they listened to Joey's voice flow out of the speakers permeating the amphitheater. Kendra felt content, combined with a deep love in her heart as she watched Joey sing.

"Tonight," Joey said before his final song. "There is someone from my past here that is very special to me. One night when I was on the road and feeling low, I thought of her and I sat down and wrote this song. I've never sang it on stage before. I think it will touch her heart. It's about a place we both dearly love. I want to sing that song for you and for her." He looked at Kendra. "Tonight as my final song, here is, Alfaland.

The auditorium quieted in anticipation. The band began to play, and Joey sang.

Alfaland

Whenever I pass a group of pines it sparks my memory
My thoughts go back to Alfaland, the place I long to be.
Wherever on earth I find myself and feel a gentle breeze
My mind wanders back to Alfaland the place I long to see.

Alfaland, sweet Alfaland, my soul cries out for thee
To see the one I love again and hold her tenderly.

Whenever I see a blooming flower it ignites a thought to me
My heart goes back to Alfaland the place I long to be.
When I hear the chirping birds singing merrily in the trees
My heart goes back to Alfaland the place I long to be.

Alfaland, sweet Alfaland, my soul cries out for thee
To see the one I love again and hold her tenderly.

When October returns and I see the changing of the leaves
My heart goes back to Alfaland the place I long to be.
When I see snow blanketing across the fields and the trees
My mind drifts back to Alfaland the place I long to see.

My heart goes back to Alfaland the place I long to be
Alfaland, sweet Alfaland, my soul cries out for thee.
To see the one I love again and hold her tenderly.

Kendra listened to the words of this cherished song. How could she have not known? It broke her heart to think that she had brought sadness or hurt to Joey.

Their eyes met several times while Joey was singing. Kendra confessed to herself that she desired to love Joey and to make him happy, to be complete and one with him. But, in the back of her mind she had many fears that she tried not to hear. "How could we ever make this work? We're now in two different worlds," she thought. She glanced around at the cheering crowd. "How could I ever take Joey away from this? His voice is too beautiful not to share it with the world. But, I can't just leave and go with him, not with the kids. Ian, Jared Jr. and Aimee Leigh could never live in this world, even if I could."

Kendra realized that love for them may have come too late and that they may have passed that opportunity ten years ago. "How different things might have been. How can I feel so good and so bad at the same time?" she thought. "There's no way I can walk away from him, and no way can I stay." She felt torn.

Joey closed his performance and then turned and ran off the side of the stage. The crowd stood in jubilant applause.

Danny tapped Kendra on the arm and motioned for her to follow. They exited through the stage door, nearly in a run, following Joey and several others down a long dark hallway. Joey grabbed her hand and they exited out a side door of the building.

Several fans were already assembled against a rope that had been secured in order to give Joey a way to the limousine parked near the door. Danny ran ahead and got the door for them and Joey and Kendra slipped inside. The vehicle sped off, leaving the crowd of disappointed fans behind.

The limousine drove off into the warm Tampa night and the two old friends and lovers embraced. They were alone, finally, except for the driver.

Joey kissed her over and over again. "Today is a dream come true for me and I swear I'll never let you go again."

"Oh Joey, I feel like my heart is going to explode." Kendra knew she needed to bring up her fears about their future. But, how could she?

"If we are going to have dinner alone and in peace, we'll have to go to my hotel room, if that's alright with you," Joey said.

"That would be fine," she said.

"Alone at last," Joey said after they were in his room.

"I feel like celebrating," Kendra said. "Do you realize this is the first we have been alone all week?"

Joey poured them both a glass of champagne. "This has been ten years on hold. He stared into her eyes.

Kendra took a sip of her champagne, "I love you so much, Joey."

"We've both experienced a lot over the last ten years," Joey said, "which makes me appreciate you even more."

"It does me too, Joey."

"What we share has gone through the fire and it is still alive more than ever." Joey took her in his arms. "I almost get jealous when I think of anyone else ever sharing your love, even Aaron," Joey said. "I never would admit that to myself before, but it's true. But, I can tell you one thing, no one has ever loved you more than I do."

"Joey, I was so lonely when I met Jared. I needed someone so bad and he was there."

"I could hate him for what he's done to you, and to us," Joey said, "and when I think I sent him to you."

"I get jealous of all the beautiful young women you've had around you," Kendra said lowering her head.

Joey placed his fingers under her chin and lifted her lips to his. "I love you. Give me a chance to show you."

"Joey, I don't know. It breaks my heart to say this, but I don't see any way. I do love you so." Kendra stroked the back of his head.

His fingers touched her shoulders. "You know, Kendra, I've been thinking about an idea for us. Sharing my life with you is more important than anything to me. Do you believe that?"

Kendra nodded and kissed his neck. "Yes, but how?"

"I've always had this dream of opening my own night club somewhere. How would you feel about building one on the south end of Alfaland? There are already several tourist attractions like, Amish Acres and Dutch Village in that area and we would be near Notre Dame and South Bend, Chicago, Fort Wayne and Indianapolis. We could probably do very well. Let the people come to me for a change. I like that thought." He looked at her, "What do you think?"

"Joey, that's a fantastic idea!" She threw her arms around his neck. "I was so concerned how we could make this work. I love it. We could even call it Alfaland." She began to kiss his face and neck.

"Then, you'll marry me?" Joey asked.

"Oh yes, Joey, yes." She was ecstatic with joy. "We will work this out," she said "I can't live my life without you, Joey."

Joey's cell phone rang. He answered it. He sat down on a chair. "That's okay," he said, "what's going on?"

Kendra stood beside him, stroking the back of his neck as he talked.

"We'll let you know shortly," Joey said. "I'll talk to Kendra and we'll get right back with you." Joey laid down the phone.

"What is it?" Kendra asked.

He looked at her and she could tell something was wrong. "Kendra, it's your sister." He placed his hand on her shoulder. "She's taken an overdose of," he shook his head, "oddly, of sleeping pills.

Kendra's eyes filled with tears. Joey pulled her near him and held her in his arms.

"How bad is it?" she asked.

"She's unconscious, but they believe she'll pull out of it. She didn't take that many, so under normal circumstances they are sure she would, but due to her past coma they can't be sure. Apparently, your father phoned Annie and she contacted Danny. He stroked the back of her head. "Do you want to go home? I can fly you in my jet. That's what Danny wanted to know."

"Yes, but I have to get the kids." She thought for a moment. "We have to pack and clean up the place. I can't just leave." She said. "I don't know what to do."

"Danny said he and Elvis would go get the kids and Annie and bring them tomorrow if we wanted to go ahead and go now." Joey touched her chin. "Kendra, I have plenty of people to help take care of that. You don't have to worry. They'll take care of everything."

"Yes, I need to go to her now Joey." She looked into his eyes, "Oh God, she can't die without peace between us. Even though everybody told me to stay away I should have talked to her. I should have tried harder."

Joey punched the button on the phone and contacted Danny.

The pilot along with one of Joey's bodyguards, and his wife went with them on the flight to Fort Akers. Joey had ordered some salads and a pizza for them to take with them since they didn't have their dinner at the motel.

"I wish there was something I could do to help," Joey said. They had finished eating and sat together on the seat in the plane. Joey had his arm around her and she had her head on his shoulder.

"Your being here is the best help in the world," Kendra said. "Can you believe all that's happened to us, Joey? Life is so unpredictable." She turned her head and looked at him. "I'm just so thankful you're with me now."

"So am I, Kendra." He kissed her on the forehead. "I feel complete when I'm with you."

"I know what you mean," She smiled, "I feel the same."

They had landed at Fort Akers Airport, by five in the morning rented a car and were soon pulling into the parking lot of the hospital.

To their amazement, Aimee Sue was awake and sitting up when they slipped into the room. It was apparent that they had interrupted a serious conversation. Byron and Jane were sitting on opposite sides of Aimee's bed, each holding one of Aimee's hands in theirs.

Kendra hesitated and stopped half way through the door, unsure whether to proceed. She did then enter the room. "Could I speak to Aimee alone?" she asked.

"Aimee and I need to talk."

Aimee looked at her but didn't speak.

Byron nodded, and they all left the room, including Joey.

Aimee Sue stared at her big sister.

"Aimee, we've got to get this worked out. We can't go on like this. It's hard on both of us and the family too."

"I know," Aimee said. "But, I can't get certain things out of my mind."

"I know exactly what you're talking about, Aimee. Don't you think I've had the same thoughts? I sat by your bed, after Jared was shot, wondering. Wondering what relationship he had, had with you. Wondering if he chose me, as his second choice after he lost you, if he was just using me to be near you? All sorts of crazy things ran through my mind. Don't you think I suffered too? I lived with him for eight years, Aimee."

"But," Aimee said. "You have everything."

"I've lost a lot too, Aimee. As a matter of fact, I lost Joey. When Jared came along, he swept me off my feet. I was week and lonely, and foolish. He was handsome and charismatic.

"He was," Aimee agreed.

"If there is someone to blame in all this, it is Jared. Don't let what he did steal our bond we once had. We both made some pretty bad mistakes, too. I've had to think so often of what Dad always said about sin being malignant, like a cancer. It grows and affects everyone around it. That's happened to us, Aimee. We knew better."

Aimee put her head down.

"But, you know what? I've forgiven Jared. He did us wrong but he paid dearly for it. He gave his life because of it."

"He did, didn't he? Aimee said. "I never thought of it that way."

"There came a point," Kendra said. "When I had to quit feeling sorry for myself and go on. I ask forgiveness from God, for any part I had in all this, and, that's what you have to do. Get up, shake yourself off and go on. Think of it this way. You've been given life back. Don't be a fool and toss it out. Can you understand what I'm saying?"

Aimee looked at her. "As a matter of fact, yes, I do. You're right. I almost made a terrible mistake. God gave me back my life, and I…I almost…I'm so ashamed. I've been so foolish. Aimee Sue stared at her big sister for a moment and then lifted her hands. She smiled and motioned for Kendra to come near. Kendra felt a combination of relief and joy. With outstretched arms and tears in her eyes, she rushed toward the welcome arms of her younger sister, whose eyes were also filled with tears. Kendra and Aimee Sue embraced and wept joyfully.

"Kendra, please forgive me. I am sorrier than you can ever know. I realize now that I was such a fool. I have so much to live for. I was given my life back and all I could concentrate on was what I'd lost.

But, I realize now that you've suffered as much, if not more, than I have. Kendra, can you ever forgive me?"

"Aimee," Kendra said, "There's nothing to forgive. We unintentionally hurt each other. We were both victims in this. I swear Aimee, I never had a clue."

"I know," Aimee said. "Kendra, I've made peace with this, and I know you understand...I've made peace with Jared. I don't know what he was thinking or why he did, what he did but I can live with it and go on."

Kendra took Aimee's hand in hers. "I know what you mean. Like I said, I've made peace with it too and am very ready to go on."

Byron stuck his head in the door. "Is everything all right in here?" he asked.

"Come on in, Dad." Aimee said, and motioned for him. "You can all come back in."

Mr. Patton walked around the bed and put his arm around Kendra and took Aimee's hand.

"We've been having a very in depth discussion, Dad." Aimee said, and my eyes are finally open. I've been such a fool. I'd like to learn to know my son and share in his life if he'll allow me to. You've done such a good job of raising him, Kendra."

"You've been no more a fool then I have," Kendra said, "and believe me, there is plenty of love in that young man of yours to share with both of us. He'll be very pleased I know."

There wasn't a dry eye in the room as the Patton family was reunited once again.

Byron embraced Joey and patted him on the back. "It's great to see you, Joey. Does this mean you'll be here for Christmas, I hope?"

"I plan to be here for all future Christmases." Joey smiled. "I love your daughter very much." He looked at Kendra. "I always have."

Byron smiled. "I had a suspicion that was the way it was, Joey. I wish I'd have told Kendra my thoughts before she got involved with Jared." He glanced over at Aimee who showed no reaction at the mention of Jared's name. "It may have spared a lot of hurt for us all."

"You know," Kendra said. "The biggest lesson that I have learned in all of this is that none of us are immune to bad things happening. To be honest, back before Aaron and mom were killed, I had the idea that I was special somehow, that bad things happened to other people. I know now that is not true."

"We've all learned a lot," Byron said.

Jane wiped her eyes with her fingers. "I believe this is going to be the best Christmas ever." Jane smiled amongst her tears.

"The children will be coming home tomorrow," Joey said.

"We only have four days to get things ready at Alfaland." Kendra smiled at Aimee in excitement at the prospect of her sharing the holiday with them.

"We'll be ready," Joey said. "I don't believe I've ever been so looking forward to Christmas. I've always envied the happiness in this family."

Joey and Kendra left the hospital and headed out to Alfaland to open up the house and get ready for the rest of the family. The sun was just coming up and the air was brisk and cold; quite an adjustment from the Florida sunshine. The ground was blanketed with a good eight inches of fresh white fluffy snow.

They disrupted the snow with their footprints and made their way to the back door. Buster came running from the barn barking. Both Kendra and Joey felt a completeness that they'd never known.

"I feel so at home here," Joey said, looking down over the pond. "I've always felt like I had no home, if you know what I mean."

"You are at home here, Joey, if you like," Kendra smiled at him.

"I like, sweetheart. Wait a minute," Joey said after she had unlocked the door. He picked her up in his arms. "I've always dreamed of doing this, Ms. Patton, Marshall, Bradley, and…" he kissed her cheek. "Now, Dubious." He carried her through the doorway at Alfaland.

Chapter Twenty-Two

*We invite you to be with us
as we begin our new life together
on Friday, the 4th of February
Two Thousand and Five
at Six Thirty in the Evening*

*Redwood Chapel
Fort Akers, Indiana*

*Kendra L. Bradley
and
Joseph G. Dubois*

*Please join us for a dinner reception
immediately following the ceremony
at Redwood Inn*

The wedding took place in a small octagon-shaped chapel built on a minute hill just southwest of Fort Akers, near the cemetery where Jared was buried.

The chapel, a small building with windows all the way around had an open ceiling that came together to create a small round steeple like dome in the center. Only a freestanding fireplace on the west side of the building heated it.

Attending were close family members and friends, including Sarah and Judy, Carmon and her family, employees from the *Fort Akers Co. Gazette*, members of Joey's band, bodyguards and their wives.

Standing proudly as Kendra's maid of honor was Aimee Sue Patton, and standing equally proud, as a bridesmaid was little Aimee Leigh. Standing with Joey were Danny, Elvis, Ian and Jared, Jr.

The ceremony was a simple one, but beautiful. Especially moving was the moment when each of the children lit a candle from an original one that Joey and Kendra had lit at the beginning of the ceremony. It brought a tear to the eye of many in the small group.

At the reception Elvis managed to take his seat beside Aimee Sue, who had been putting on weight, gaining strength and looking and feeling great. "Joey didn't tell me Kendra had such a beautiful sister," he stated.

Aimee looked at him and smiled. "You could say I've been out of circulation for quite some time." She was glad he had sat down beside her. Aimee had seen him around with Joey a few times, but had not yet had the opportunity to speak with him. She went on to explain to him about being in the coma for the past eight years. "I feel like I've just come back to life in the last couple of months."

He was captivated by her story. "That's amazing," he said. "I've never heard of anything like it, except maybe in the movies."

"You look fantastic."

Thank you, I feel good," Aimee said, "That's my son Ian over at the banquet table." She pointed toward Ian. "Kendra, thankfully, took him in and raised him as her own all these years. We are just slowly getting to know each other. I am so proud of him. It's a little difficult to grasp that he's my son and likewise for him. He is going to continue to live with Kendra and Joey at Alfaland for now. He considers that his family and I understand. Maybe sometime down the road..." She smiled. "Who knows? Right now, I'm planning on finishing my education and enjoying this return to life that I've been given."

"I didn't realize Ian wasn't Kendra's boy," he said, "He and Jared look so much alike."

Aimee decided to change the subject. "Your name is Elvis, that's unique," she said.

"My parents were Elvis fans, what can I say?" He laughed. "It's been interesting to live with."

Before the reception ended, Elvis asked Aimee, "Would it be all right if I called you and we could see each other again?"

"I'd like that," Aimee said.

That day was the beginning of a lasting relationship between Aimee Sue and Elvis Elliott. The following year, another wedding took place at the same chapel with the same group attending.

The year also brought about changes at Alfaland. Joey had some obligations that he had to fulfill, so during May and June Kendra went on tour with him. The kids spent the first month traveling with Byron and Jane, and during the second month Aimee Sue stayed with them at Alfaland. Later in the year, with Elvis's help, Joey began building his nightclub at the south end of Alfaland. A new member joined their family in December when Hanna Lynn Dubois was born.

"You know," Joey said as he sat by Kendra's bed holding his new daughter. "This is happiness. This is where it's at. No amount of money or fame or things can bring such joy." His eyes glassed over. "I love you and our family so much."

Kendra stroked Hanna's head and then touched Joey's cheek and smiled. "This is where it's at. I love you too, Joey."